ONE ROTTEN APPLE

LYNDIE LAVENDER
COZY MYSTERY 1

PENNY FROST MCGINNIS

Cozy Beacon Press

ISBN: 979-8-9944720-0-2

Published in the United States of America

Cover Art watercolor painting and design: Maggie Wickline-Jowers

This is a work of fiction. All of the names, characters, organizations, and incidents portrayed in this novel are products of the author's imagination and are used in a fictitious situation. Any resemblances to actual persons, living or dead, events, locales, or incidents are coincidental and not the intent of the author. Any mistakes are the authors.

Contents

Dedication

To Bev, Jackie, Kim, and Kathleen, who encouraged me and helped me shape this story. Thank you for believing I could learn a new genre and write this book.

The Lord is my shepherd, I lack nothing.
He makes me lie down in green pastures,
he leads me beside quiet waters,
he refreshes my soul.
He guides me along the right paths
for his name's sake.
Even though I walk
through the darkest valley,
I will fear no evil,
for you are with me;
your rod and your staff,
they comfort me.
Psalm 23:1-4 (NIV)

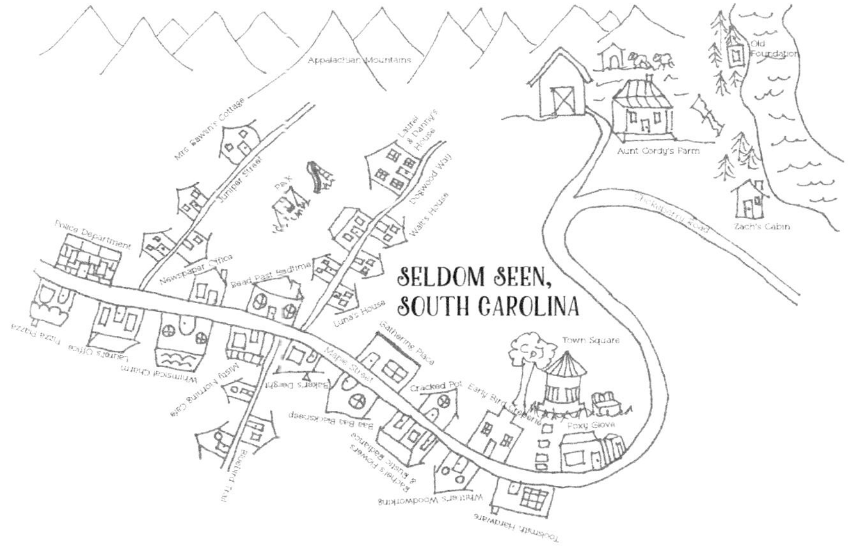
SELDOM SEEN,
SOUTH CAROLINA
Appalachian Mountains
Old Foundation
Aunt Cordy's Farm
Zach's Cabin
Mrs Rawlin's Cottage
Juniper Street
Park
Laurel & Danny's House
Dogwood Way
Walt's House
Luna's House
Police Department
Newspaper Office
Read Past Bedtime
Pizza Piazza
Laurel's Office
Whimsical Charm
Misty Morning Cafe
Baker's Delight
Bluebird Trail
Maple Street
Gathering Place
Baa Baa Blacksheep
Rachel's Flowers & Rustic Radiance
Cracked Pot
Early Bird Creperie
Town Square
Foxy Glove
Whitaker's Woodworking
Toolsmith Hardware

Penny Frost McGinnis

Characters:

Lyndie Lavender: *Former war correspondent and photojournalist now lives on her Aunt Cordy's homestead*

Cordelia Benton: *Aunt Cordy to Lyndie and Laurel*

Laurel Armstrong: *Lyndie's sister, runs the Seldom Seen blog*

Danny Armstrong: *Laurel's husband and local police officer*

Josephine Armstong: *Laurel and Danny's daughter*

Henry Armstrong: *Laurel and Danny's son*

Zach Hudson: *New to the area naturalist and tenant of Aunt Cordy*

Arthur Richardson: *Mayor of Seldom Seen, SC*

Walt Jenkins: *Aunt Cordy's beau*

Otis Reardon: *Owner of Toolsmith Hardware*

Janine Oliver: *Owner of Read Past Bedtime Book Shop*

Delight Brooks: *Owner of Delight's Bakery*

Jonquil Rose: *Owner of Baa Baa Black Sheep Yarn Shop*

Marcy Fox: *Owner of The Foxy Glove Boutique*

June Bower: *Former mayor's assistant*

Leo Randolph: *Woodworker and business owner*

Greg Garrison: *New to town mystery man*

Johnson Winters: *New to town handyman*

Chapter One

Saturday morning, my aunt, sister, and I hustled to prepare for the opening weekend of Aunt Cordy's annual Autumn Apple Fest.

October's morning light filtered through golden, tangerine, and scarlet leaves. Autumn beauty colored the foothills of the Appalachian Mountains, where my aunt made her livelihood on a South Carolina homestead. The apple orchard produced in abundance this fall, my first autumn back in twenty years.

My aunt's new tenant, Zach Hudson, and I positioned long wooden tables in the food truck area away from the petting zoo. Those two smells didn't need to mix.

My aunt loved this day, and I wanted to make everything perfect for her. "Hey, Zach." I grabbed one of the red checkered tablecloths, snapping and shaking it out. "How about I spread these out, and you can follow me, centering the mums and bittersweet on the tables?"

My sister, Laurel, and her hubby, Police Officer Danny Armstrong, worked like busy bees and placed the folding chairs around the eating area. I had to smile at their kiddos, Josephine and Henry, who fed the animals in the mini-petting zoo. They chased Aunt Cordy's chickens, while her Nigerian Dwarf goats, Bashful and Happy, *baaed* at them.

Billowing clouds hung in the bluest sky and set a glorious backdrop for the festivities. A perfect seventy-degrees promised a comfortable day for the many folks we expected. People from all over upstate South Carolina came for my aunt's apples, apple butter, apple jelly, and her delicious apple stack cake, as well as to browse the vendors from our town who offered a variety of wares.

"Lyndie Louise Lavender, can you come help me, please?" My aunt seldom called me by my full name or raised her voice unless she needed my help, or I'd done something egregious. She stood on the porch step and held an enamel roasting pan filled with water deep enough to bob for apples. I scurried to her and clutched one side. We carried the pan, at the speed of a turtle, to a booth and rested it on a low table.

Aunt Cordy rubbed her lower back. "Thank you. Can you toss seven or eight of the Pink Lady apples into the pan? We don't want too many at a time."

"Sure, but aren't they harder to bite into?" I lifted a bag of reddish apples from a wooden crate.

"No use making the game easy. Don't want to hand out all the prizes at once." She winked and sauntered away.

After I dropped the shiny red apples into the pan, I scattered small stuffed animals, beaded bracelets, and bouncy balls on the prize table. When Zach wasn't teaching the story of Johnny Appleseed in the orchard, we planned to take turns supervising the kids bobbing for apples. We supplied the booth with paper towels for the folks who soaked their heads and clothes after they dunked for an apple and earned their cheap freebie. My dad would have said, "All in good fun," if he were here instead of in Guatemala, where he and my mom still served as missionaries and teachers.

My sister Laurel and I had spent many summers and times our family traveled home for furlough with our aunt. Now, after twenty years of serving as a photojournalist in several war zones, I'd returned to my favorite place on earth, Seldom Seen, South Carolina, a small town in the foothills of the Appalachian Mountains. My weary eyes had witnessed so much devastation and death, so now I relished the quiet life on my aunt's homestead. Days spent side by side with Aunt Cordy in the apple orchard had offered a respite from the sorrow I had experienced.

She had warned me in September that Autumn Apple Fest would interrupt the solitude. I'd prayed for energy and strength to tackle the preparation, even while I expected to have a fun time. The folks from town had welcomed me, since they adored my aunt. Over the months I had lived in her upstairs I'd discovered a feeling I'd not experienced in years. Home. Her small stick-built house with a cozy porch embraced me and rooted me. With Laurel and her family nearby, my heart overflowed.

By nine o'clock, car after car meandered onto Aunt Cordy's gravel driveway and parked in the grassy field. Neighbors, townsfolk, and strangers wandered the booths as a breeze whispered through the air. I manned the apple-bobbing booth and witnessed a brother and sister fight over the same apple. Little sister's face dove in then rose triumphant with the skin of the rosy apple between her teeth. I congratulated her and offered her a stuffed red panda. She handed the animal to her younger brother, and they both walked away with a smile.

Aunt Cordy, in the booth beside me, traded jar after jar of her apple butter and jelly for dollars. The loaves of apple bread and her delicious stacked apple cakes sold out in the first two hours.

"Good morning, Mayor Richardson." He approached the booth in his jeans and red flannel shirt. The sun reflected off his bald head.

"Hello, Lyndie. Your aunt has outdone herself, as usual. I bet she's happy to have your help. And that new fellow, Zach. He's a naturalist, right?" He stepped past me and grabbed an apple from the basket at the back of the booth.

I reloaded the apple-bobbing tub. "Yes, Zach teaches nature classes at the outdoor education center and for whoever else asks. He's been a big help to Aunt Cordy since he's been living in her rental cabin."

"Good to hear." The mayor nodded, then turned and walked away. Three more kids ran to my booth and tried their best to bite into an apple. Before they accomplished their goal, voices rose from two booths down. Otis Reardon, owner of Toolsmith Hardware, raised his fist and shouted at Mayor Richardson. "Just watch. You're out here schmoozing to win the election. I've got solid backing, and plenty of people will vote for me. Don't think you're a shoo-in, 'cause you're not."

Mayor Richardson shuffled back a step. "Now Otis, no need to get riled. I'm sure it'll be a fair race. Besides, the actual election isn't until next year." He patted Otis on the shoulder. "You're a good guy, but you aren't mayor material." He chuckled. "Listen to you. Yelling at me. Tsk, tsk." He strutted to the Early Bird Creperie food truck.

Zach slid into our booth. "What's going on with those two?"

I shrugged. "Otis plans to put his hat in the ring for mayor, and Arthur Richardson needles Otis and gets him upset. Two days ago, in town, they yelled at each other about the sidewalk in front of Toolsmith Hardware. Otis says the town is responsible, and the mayor says the store owner holds the responsibility of repairing the cement. I have no idea who is right."

Zach handed paper towels to two of the children who caught apples in their teeth. "I'm not sure I'd vote for either one."

"I'm with you, but I'm not sure either of us has lived here long enough to cast a vote." Movement caught my attention. "Here comes Danny with fresh water for the bobbing pot. Seeing everyone stick their faces in the same water makes my stomach squirm. I keep thinking about the number of germs swimming in the pan. I witnessed way worse in the war zones, but now I'm going soft."

"I get it. I'm not one to share food or drinks with anyone." He dumped the other pan of water. After Danny placed the fresh pot on the table, Zach handed him the empty one. We'd made it halfway through the day.

Laurel scurried to our tent and stepped inside. "Did you hear the ruckus a few minutes ago?"

Her husband, Danny, squeezed Laurel's hand. "We all heard the mayor and Otis. They were fussing about the upcoming election that's a year away. Don't pay them any mind." My brother-in-law served the town as an officer of the law, and his no-nonsense attitude spilled into Laurel's daily life.

My sister gave him her "I know" stare. "It's ridiculous they argue in public when they want our votes, but honey, I get it. I was only talking to you three." She pivoted in my direction. "When are you taking photos for my blog? I want to promote the next two weekends for Aunt Cordy."

Laurel ran the *Come See What's in Seldom Seen* promotional blog to keep folks in tune with what our little town offered. "Zach is free until later this afternoon, so I'll snap photos between now and then."

"Sounds good, Sis. I need to get to my booth. I'm handing out pamphlets with a list of the businesses we have in town and the services they offer, plus a map of the festival. Stop and see me, Lyndie." Danny wrapped his hand around hers, and they strolled across the main thoroughfare.

Several children and adults formed a line for apple bobbing. "Do you need me to stay and help?"

Zach pulled his shoulder-length brown hair into a ponytail and tucked a strand behind his ear. "Nah. I've got this. You go take pictures, or your sister will get after you."

I extracted my camera from the bag I'd stashed in a box in the booth and wrapped the multicolored strap around my neck. "She pays me to help her, so I best not complain. I'll be back."

Thirteen booths plus the petting zoo, the cut your own sunflowers tent, and the food truck roundup filled the field in front of Aunt Cordy's house. She'd organized this event for ten years and welcomed the people with a joy-filled heart. I surveyed the activities and groups gathered at each vendor as I sought out photo ops.

Jonquil Rose had set up her weaving and yarn booth, Baa Baa Black Sheep. Her variegated yarns through my camera lens dazzled like a rainbow. The sweet, snow-white lamb she had with her curled at her feet as she wove threads across a small loom. I grew to love sheep on my forays overseas. The mountain people I had met kept flocks. The gentle sheep had let me pet them when I photographed them and their shepherds. Laurel would love the photos of Jonquil and her lamb.

I aimed my camera at the hand-dyed cotton threads. Later, I'd circle back to purchase rich shades of crimson, indigo, and gold for my current embroidery project. Women I'd encountered overseas had taught me to stitch and create artistic designs. The women in India had sewn quilts called kanthas from scrap material and embellished them with vibrant embroidery. The colorful birds and flowers inspired me.

Rachel of Rachel's Flowers handed out nosegays with her business cards and sold bouquets and small bowls of succulents. I caught her on camera with a broad smile handing a bouquet to

Walt, my aunt's friend. Wonder who he bought those for? Aunt Cordy denied any more than friendship, but Laurel and I had our own ideas.

An array of books on wooden library carts filled Janine Oliver's Read Past Bedtime Booth. "You have a book sale."

Janine held a children's storybook. "A sale and story time. I'm hoping to promote the store and draw in more parents. Storytime starts in a few minutes. I have several picture books and chapter books for the parents to peruse while I read to the kids. We'll see what happens. I'd love to have more children in the store." Janine had tied her long red hair back with a pink bandanna, and her flowing dress, sprinkled with wildflowers, swayed around her legs. The kids would love her. I envied her free spirit. When the little ones gathered, I snapped photos, with the parents' permission. They oohed and awed as Janine read the story. I even caught a photo of Aunt Cordy's Bernese Mountain Dog, Murphy, listening to the story. Perfect for the blog.

The smell of baked bread and sweets drew me to the next booth. Delight Brooks, the owner of Baker's Delight, offered samples of her sourdough bread. An array of donuts, muffins, and scones filled the portable counter. I purchased a cranberry-orange scone, and the first bite melted in my mouth.

Before I shot more photos, I stopped and checked on Aunt Cordy. Walt stood beside her and helped her take money for apple bags. Several folks purchased bags from her and then picked and filled their bags with as many apples as they could fit from the orchard. I snapped a photo of the two of them and captured the beautiful fall bouquet he'd purchased with sunflowers and purple asters. Walt was a sweetheart who blessed my aunt.

On the opposite end of the field, Marcy Fox had several colorful sweaters hanging in The Foxy Glove booth. The sole boutique in town carried everything from hiking boots to fancy dresses. She wore jeans the color of rust and a violet, rust, and cream striped sweater. Johnson Winters, who moved to town about the time I did, chatted with Marcy. Her eyelids fluttered, and her mouth bowed into a smile. Both in their sixties, the flirting between the two tickled me. Johnson picked up handyman jobs. He'd repaired the roof on Aunt Cordy's barn over the summer. Seemed nice enough, but he kept to himself, except around Marcy. When a customer came to the booth, I photographed Marcy showing off a teal sweater while Mr. Winters loitered in the background.

When I returned to the apple bobbing booth, Zach hurried to the storytelling area in the orchard to talk about Johnny Appleseed again. An hour later, my analog watch—yes old-fashioned of me—turned to five o'clock and the festival ended for the day. Vendors packed away their items, and by six o'clock they rolled off the property.

Weariness invited Aunt Cordy, Laurel, Walt, and I to plop into the Adirondack chairs around the fire pit, while Danny and Zach laid logs for a fire. I waited for the heat of the flames to warm my toes, as I flipped through the photos on my camera. Not bad. I'd captured the energy and joy of the day.

Tomorrow the festivities opened at noon. We'd have time to go to church before we welcomed another crowd. Even though my toes froze and fatigue settled into my body, the energy of the day left me restless. I rose from the wooden chair. "I'm heading to the river to capture photos of the sunset. Anyone else want to come with me?"

"I will." Our local naturalist brushed dirt from his hands.

Zach, Murphy, and I hiked around Aunt Cordy's sunflower patch across the meadow to the wooded river path. He held a low tree limb so it wouldn't smack me in the face. "Thanks for coming."

"I don't pass on walks or hikes." We cut across a dirt path.

"What did you think of your first day at the Apple Fest?"

"I was amazed at the number of people in attendance." We drew closer to the river. "As much as I enjoyed myself, the disagreement between the mayor and Otis bugged me. Are they always so disrespectful to each other?" Zach pointed to a rock in the trail. "Be careful."

The mayor and Otis had disrupted the joy of the day. Why did two grown men act like toddlers fighting over a toy? As we approached the remnants of foundational stones and half walls from a home built in the 1800s, the ugly blot on the day left an uneasiness in my gut.

On the river's edge, my eyes adjusted to the light filtering through the trees and the wispy fog floating from the river. Even as the river's song soothed my soul, an eerie sense of dread settled with the fog like a shadow.

Chapter Two

Erosion and time had chipped away at the wall built of limestone, a place once called home. Aunt Cordy believed a family had constructed the ramshackle building along the riverbank for the natural water source. In the months I'd lived here, I'd found the perch a calm and solitary spot to read and take photos. Not today. On this day in October, Zach, Murphy, and I ambled across the pasture to the river's edge where the fog played hide and seek.

"Moving to your aunt's property turned out to be a true blessing. With the river and woods, plus the meadows, I've had a chance to study the wildlife and plants. Plus, it's peaceful." Zach knelt and petted Murphy.

"I love it here, especially along the river. I've photographed several great blue herons, green herons, and egrets. They're fun to watch and make great photo subjects."

"I'd love to see your photos. They have a rookery nearby where they've built nests."

"Aunt Cordy pointed it out to me when I came home. She's quite knowledgeable about the area."

Zach stood and pointed at a rabbit that skittered away from us. "The deer aren't shy either. One came to my porch the other day."

"Have you seen the remnants of the old home on the riverbank?"

"I noticed it but haven't explored it."

The sun's rays dimmed as we approached the remains of the old stone walls. I stepped through what was left of the doorway and my foot caught on a root. Except it wasn't a root. I stumbled and fell—on top of Mayor Richardson. A knot twisted in my stomach, and a scream stuck in my throat. Squeamishness threatened to overtake me. Zach offered his hand, and I pushed from the ground.

"He's not moving." My voice shook as I knelt beside the mayor and placed my fingers on his wrist. "Zach there's no pulse. Call Danny and 911."

"Is he dead?" Zach's whisper echoed louder than the crows' caw.

"Probably."

By second nature, I forced compressions to the tune of *Staying Alive*. Nothing. His pale skin against the dirt sent waves of sorrow through me. The rush of the river rolled in my ears. A few hours ago, we'd conversed. He had perused the festival and schmoozed the people. A dark purple bruise spread on his neck, and blood pooled under his head. Did he fall? Perhaps he walked to the river and tripped, except he lay face up. Did someone hit him? I gave up on the compressions. His coloring revealed it was far too late for life-saving measures. Out of habit, from my years of photojournalism, I snapped photos of his neck and body and the surroundings.

I stepped back beside Zach and waited for Danny. Murphy crouched at my side. The whooshing rustling of footsteps in the field announced his arrival. He darted past us and knelt beside the body. Again, the words *no pulse* filled the silence. Not even a bird chirped for several seconds. When he finished talking into his radio, Danny approached Zach and me. "Are you guys okay?"

"I'm alright." I hugged my arms to myself and glanced at Zach. I'd witnessed a lot of death in my job, but not usually someone I knew. Yes, a few of my colleagues had died in the war zones, but no one I had spent much time with, except for one. My eyes watered.

"I'm okay." The naturalist nodded. No doubt in his line of work he'd experienced the death of animals, but probably not people.

Danny pulled out a notebook and a pencil, something he carried with him everywhere. "You both need to tell me what you saw once we get this cordoned off. When the other officers arrive, we'll comb the area and decide if this was an accident. He may have fallen, but I can't say for sure." He jotted notes on the paper. "In the meantime, go to the house and wait."

Before we hiked to the house, I glanced at the mayor and whispered a prayer for those who would miss him. No matter who the person was, death was hard.

Danny tapped me on the shoulder. "You can tell Cordy and Laurel, but no one else, and Walt if he's still here. Otherwise, keep it quiet."

"Will do." Zach and I trekked along the path to the house. The golden meadow no longer held the charm of the trip to the river. As the sun lowered in the sky, Danny and the officers faced a long night. Weariness weighed on my shoulders and my steps.

Zach's hand landed on my shoulder with a light tap. "You doing okay?"

My mouth curved into a small smile. "Yeah, but it's weird when it's someone you know."

"Same." He cleared his throat. "I noticed you took photos."

I hugged the camera to me. "Yeah. It's ingrained in me after twenty years of photojournalism. Maybe something will help the police if this wasn't an accident."

Zach stopped and stared at me. His eyebrows furrowed, and he tilted his head to the side. "Not an accident? Why would you say that?"

I shrugged. "I take nothing for granted after what I've seen. Most likely he fell and hit his head, but the police investigation will tell us." The bruise on the neck and the sight of the blood burned an unwanted picture into my brain.

"O-kay." He pursed his lips, and we kept walking.

Once we reached the yard, we jogged to the fire pit and found empty chairs. From around the corner, Josephine and Henry's laughter sang out. Quite a contrast to what we had witnessed. Zach and I trudged to the porch and Murphy darted toward the barn. The fatigue in my legs left each step heavier than the next. The news we had to share left my stomach in turmoil. Aunt Cordy and Laurel listened to Walt as he strummed the guitar. A beautiful moment about to be marred.

Laurel lifted her head and looked me dead in the eyes. "What's going on? Danny's phone rang, then he tore across the field toward the river."

"You don't miss a beat, do you, sister?" I lowered myself into the chair beside her, and Zach leaned on the porch rail. "You might want to make sure the kids can't hear."

She called the kids to the porch and sent them inside for a snack, then squinted at me. "What's going on?"

Zach and I exchanged a glance. I turned to them and lowered my voice. "We found Mayor Richardson by the old stone walls. He's dead."

Aunt Cordy's hand flew to her mouth. Walt leaned his guitar against the wall and clasped her other hand. Laurel's mouth fell open. All expected reactions.

"We cannot mention this to anyone. Danny said to keep it among us. They need to investigate the area and figure out what happened." I stood and crossed the porch to my aunt and leaned down and hugged her. Next, I approached Laurel, held her tight, then let go and lowered into a chair before my legs gave out. The hugs helped me as much as they helped them. I'd have given anything to have Aunt Cordy's hugs every day over the last twenty years.

A loss for words hung over us as I stared at the night sky. The full moon hung in the sky with thousands of stars, too joyful for this night. Josephine and Henry broke the silence when they bounced onto the porch with milk mustaches and cookie crumbs on their shirts. Jo plopped at her momma's feet. "When can we go home? I'm tired."

Laurel patted her daughter on the shoulder. "We'd better go. Daddy will be a little later. He has some things to take care of."

"How's Daddy going to get home? He rode with us." Henry tugged Laurel's hand.

Walt stood and lifted his guitar. "I can drop you off if you don't mind riding in my '65 Ford Mustang. I drove it today to show a couple of the festivalgoers who had asked me about it." His chest puffed with pride. He distracted the kiddos and made the moment easier for Laurel.

Henry clapped. "Yes!"

"There's your answer." Laurel hustled them into the house to gather their jackets. Walt kissed Aunt Cordy on the forehead. When Laurel and the kids came out to the porch, she hugged me one more time, then they all climbed into the dream car and drove off.

Zach placed an arm around Aunt Cordy's shoulders. "Is there anything I can do for you before I head to the cabin?"

"No, but thanks for asking. You'd better get some rest. We'll wait for Danny." She side-hugged him.

His glance met mine. "You okay?"

I waved my hands in front of me. "You go on to the cabin. I'll tell Danny where you are if he needs to talk to you." His sad brown eyes searched my face. "I'm glad I wasn't alone, and don't worry about me. I'm fine." Fine. What kind of word was fine anyway? The one I say when I don't know what else to say, but don't we all give a generic reply sometimes? My body, physically exhausted, not fine. My emotional state, shaken, not fine. My spiritual state, struggling, not fine. Yet, with my sixty-something year old aunt in need of my strength, I'm fine.

Inside the house, we settled in the living room, Aunt Cordy on the sofa and me in the comfy recliner. If I flipped the footrest out, I'd fall asleep, so I crossed my legs and bobbed my foot.

My aunt shook her head. "The mayor died on my property during one of my favorite days. It's not right. Not at all." Tears trickled down her cheeks. She dabbed her face with a tissue. "I wasn't close to him. We had more of a professional relationship. He kept his private life to himself. He moved here about five years ago. A year after his arrival, he ran for mayor. The previous one had retired and moved to Arizona, and Arthur had no one to run against him. He appeared competent and got the job. He's made good changes in the town. Added much-needed public parking and planted several trees along the streets. He's tried to recapture the quaintness of Seldom Seen from the years the place thrived." She sniffed. "I have no idea if he has family or where they might be. He's been single since he lived here."

I moved to the couch and held my aunt's hand. "I'm sorry this is such a shock. If you're up to it, Danny will tell us if we can continue with the festival."

"I don't know if I can, at least not tomorrow."

Gravel crunched under tires in the driveway. I left the couch and peered out the window. "The coroner arrived. I imagine they'll move the body tonight. Do you want to get ready for bed?"

"No. I want to talk to Danny first. It's my property, and I want to know what happened." Aunt Cordy closed her eyes and curled her lips between her teeth.

"How about a cup of tea while we wait?"

She blinked. "Yes, please."

In the kitchen, I turned the heat on under the tea kettle. I retrieved two bags of Lady Grey tea from a tin and placed them in Aunt Cordy's handmade hand warmer mugs. She had thrown pottery for a few years at one of the mountain art studios and created mugs in muted red and green tones with a closed handle where we rested our fingers. I hoped the heat from the tea translated to comfort and a moment of peace.

The kettle whistled, and I poured the steaming water over the bags. A sweet, citrusy smell rose with the steam from the steeping tea. I carried the mugs to the living room and handed one to Aunt Cordy, along with a few oatmeal chocolate chip cookies my niece and nephew didn't devour. She wrapped her hands around the mug and allowed the steam to warm her face.

"Thank you, dear one. This is perfect." She sipped the tea, then creased her forehead and frowned.

"Something else on your mind?"

"When I cleaned and reorganized my booth, I gathered the apple butter paddles I had displayed, and one went missing. Did you see it anywhere?"

"You have several. Which one is missing?" I played with the string of the teabag, then tugged the bag to the top of the cup, squeezed the liquid out, and placed it on a saucer.

Aunt Cordy did the same. "The stick is about three feet long, and the paddle on the end with the holes looks yay long and is three inches thick." She held her hands out about a foot apart. "I use it for demonstrations. Tomorrow, I'd planned to show our guests the process of apple butter making." She pressed her cup to the table and snagged a cookie.

I strode to the kitchen and poked in the corners and a couple cabinets then returned to the living room and dropped into the chair. "Did Walt help carry your equipment in?"

Dark circles lingered under her eyes. "He did. I'll call him in the morning and ask if he's seen it." She nibbled the cookie.

"Why don't you lay down? I'll wait for Danny." The long day had left us both exhausted. My dry eyes itched, and my shoulders ached.

The hinges on the front door creaked as it swung open. Danny stomped his boots on the blue and gray braided rug. His six-foot two frame towered over us until he rested on the sofa beside Aunt Cordy. "Ladies."

"Danny?" My voice—a question mark.

Chapter Three

If I met Danny on the street, with his blond hair and blue eyes, I'd swear he spent his life as a surfer, but this man, raised in the mountains, carried a passion for his people. Even the ones who lived here for a short time. His forehead wrinkled as his long, tan fingers covered my aunt's hand. His heart for my sister, Laurel, and our family beat as strong as it did for the people he protected. On the rare occasions I had journeyed home in the past twenty years, he made sure Laurel and I had time to visit. Those two kids of his adored him but had no idea what he dealt with day in and day out. Seldom Seen proved quiet most of the time, but on other days, not so much. Like today.

A tightrope's tension strung across the room. Danny studied Aunt Cordy's face. What was going on? I rose from my chair and stood in front of them. "Can I get you coffee or tea?" Danny's head turned to me.

"None for me. Thanks. You'd best sit." He tugged his cell phone from his pants pocket and lit the screen. I watched him scroll. He stopped and held the phone in front of my aunt. "Do you recognize this?"

She wrapped a hand around the phone and pulled it to her face. "Of course I do. We were searching for my paddle a few minutes ago. I had it at the festival, and it disappeared. That's one of my apple butter paddles, the one I use with the big outdoor kettle. You've seen me use it." She handed the phone to him. "I'm glad you found it. I plan to use it tomorrow."

He tucked the phone into his pocket. "I'm afraid you can't."

Aunt Cordy scowled at Danny, a sight I hadn't witnessed often. She crossed her arms and stared at him. "Why not? I need it for the apple butter making demonstration."

Danny heaved a sigh. "We believe it's a murder weapon."

Aunt Cordy's eyes rounded. "What? Murder! Didn't the mayor fall and hit his head?"

"We have reason to believe someone hit Mayor Richardson with the paddle. He may have fallen and hit his head after the blow. The investigation will reveal more clues." Danny ran his hand over his short blond waves. "When was the last time you saw the paddle?"

My aunt rubbed her forehead, then reclined against the back of the couch and closed her eyes. I leaned forward, with my hands folded and my elbows resting on my legs. If I could help her think, I would. "She told me she hadn't seen it since it was in her booth at the festival."

"I didn't ask you, Lyndie. Your aunt has to answer." Danny's stern face put me in my place. I scooted back in my chair.

Aunt Cordy opened her eyes and turned to Danny. "I remember seeing it around four o'clock because I had a customer ask me what it was. It was lying across a table at the back of the booth with a few smaller ones. I carried it to the front for the woman to see, then I gave her a brief history of why the end was attached to a long stick and why the holes helped the apple butter mix and cook better. After we finished, I returned the piece to the table." She wrinkled her forehead. "I didn't set it on the table. I leaned it on the table beside the opening in the back of the booth. I assumed Walt carried it in the house when we closed, but Lyndie and I couldn't find it."

Danny jotted in his notebook. "Were you in your booth between four and five o'clock?"

"Of course I was, except when I went to the house to grab more jelly and go to the bathroom." She eyed Danny like he would a suspect.

"How long did you take?"

Aunt Cordy stood, with a hand on each hip. "Why are you asking?" She planted herself in front of the couch and crossed her arms.

Danny rose and faced her. "Since the paddle belongs to you, and your fingerprints are on it, you need an alibi." I covered a grin when his expression of *there you have it* caused Aunt Cordy's mouth to fall open. Of course, she had nothing to do with the murder. Danny had to check off his mandatory list.

My aunt had transferred spiders outside to the garden if she found them in the house. She opened the windows for flies and bees to get out. She wouldn't hurt a living creature, much less a human.

Aunt Cordy's eyes pleaded with me for help. I sensed somehow I'd end up in the middle of the mess.

She swung her gaze back at Danny. "If you must know, I ran to the house for about twenty minutes. It took a little longer in the lady's room than I expected. I forgot to eat my prunes last night." A rosy blush colored her cheeks. "When I finished, I returned to the booth with my arms loaded with jelly and apple butter. I planned to leave them in a crate for tomorrow."

"Can anyone verify your time away from the booth?"

"Well...no one was in the toilet with me, if that's what you want to know." She crossed her arms and plopped on the couch.

"Thanks, Aunt Cordy. I'll check with Walt to see what he remembers. In the meantime, don't talk to anyone else about this." Danny turned to me. "Where's Zach? I told him to stay here."

"He went to his cabin, since it's late." I saw Aunt Cordy roll her eyes. "I can call Zach and ask him to come over if you want to talk to him."

"How about you and I walk to his cabin and let Aunt Cordy get some rest?" Danny motioned to the door.

"Let me get a jacket." I took a breather as I climbed the stairs to my room. Voices sounded downstairs, but at least no one yelled. Back in the living room, Danny had an arm around Aunt Cordy's shoulders.

"I understand, Danny, but I'd never hurt anyone." Red blotches dotted her cheeks, and her eyes watered.

"I know. I'll talk to you tomorrow." He patted her back and then joined me at the door.

#####

Clouds muted the moon's light. The trees' shadows waved their arms as a chill touched my skin. Wood smoke wafted through the air. The looming mountains and owl hoots filled my head with eeriness, like something I'd experienced in the Ukraine at night in the abandoned villages.

Zach's cabin sat on the river, an eighth of a mile from the crime scene. We trekked the path through the woods to his doorstep. A small porch, big enough for two metal lawn chairs, covered the front of the log house. I knocked. Zach opened the door, and his red-rimmed eyes told me he had dozed off while he waited but hadn't rested.

"Come in. Sorry I didn't stay at the house, Danny. I wanted Cordy and Lyndie to have time together." He gestured for us to enter. "Have a seat on the couch." We settled on the flowered couch, where the corners had rubbed thin on the cushions. The scent of toasted bread reminded me I hadn't eaten this evening. Zach carried a folding chair from the kitchenette, unfolded it, and then perched on the seat. His gaze landed on Danny.

My brother-in-law again pulled out his notepad and pen. "What can you tell me about what you and Lyndie discovered?" When he said my name, he gave me the don't talk eye.

"Lyndie said she wanted to walk to the river and take some photos, so I volunteered to go with her. When we reached the foundation of the old house, Lyndie tripped. I saw Mayor

Richardson's body when I reached to help her stand. She told me to call you and 911, so I did. While she applied CPR, I prayed, and I noticed the bruise on his neck and the blood on the ground. Then we waited for you." He leaned against the back of the chair. The fireplace crackled, and warmth spread across the room.

Danny finished writing and eyed Zach. "What interactions have you had with the mayor?"

Zach cleared his throat. "Not many. My boss introduced me to him when I moved here, and he attended one of my workshops when I spoke on how to tell if a tree is unhealthy. Otherwise, I haven't seen much of him."

"Where were you between four and five o'clock this afternoon?"

He took a breath. "I was in the apple bobbing booth from four to four-thirty, then teaching about Johnny Appleseed in the orchard from four-thirty to five. At five we cleaned the booth and closed for the day."

Puzzled about the time, I tapped Danny's arm. "Why four o'clock?"

Danny gave a half-smile. "I spoke to the mayor a few minutes before four. We chatted about the festival. We all gathered at the fire pit a few minutes after five. You found him at five forty-five. I'm trying to construct a timeline. You were all with me around five. Anything else?" His expression dared me to ask. I loved Danny, but he could intimidate me when he wanted.

"Nope. No more questions from me." I settled into the cushions and hoped they'd suck me in.

Danny stood. "I don't have anything else. If I do, I'll be back."

I followed him to the door. "Goodnight, Zach."

"Night. See you tomorrow." He waved his hand.

We trod along the path in silence. Before he climbed into his car, he hugged me and asked me to take care of Aunt Cordy. A shiver of fear traveled along my spine due to his ominous tone. No way my aunt had anything to do with the mayor's death. She loved everyone, and everyone loved her.

In the house, I searched for her to say goodnight. I peeked into her bedroom, and she'd fallen asleep on the bed in her clothes, no doubt exhausted. I laid the blue and white crocheted afghan from the end of her bed over her.

#####

Sunday morning, I padded down the steps to the kitchen. Silence. No coffee brewed, and no bacon sizzled. Down the hallway, I peeked into the bedroom. She'd straightened her bed. I hurried to the living room and glanced out the window. Aunt Cordy rocked on the front porch with her Bible on her lap. Should I leave her be or check on her? I checked.

I creaked open the door. "Good morning."

Her hand landed over her heart. "You scared me. Sorry I'm jumpy this morning." She closed the Bible. "Danny texted me and asked me not to open the festival today. He's afraid people will wander to the river and nose around the crime scene. I posted on social media before I came outside, and so did Laurel. We'll have to stand at the end of the driveway and turn people away. I'm sorry for the vendors."

I sat and rocked beside her. "We have two more weekends. I'm sure they'll understand. Do we need to call the vendors this morning?"

"We do. Which means we won't get to church." She patted the Bible on her lap.

I patted her hand and stood. "I'll help make phone calls."

She squeezed my hand. "Wait."

I sat and waited. Her face paled. "Danny also said for me not to go anywhere. The only prints on the paddle are mine." She turned her face to me, and her eyes pleaded. "You've got to help me. I didn't do anything. I would never hurt anyone, but of course Danny has to follow the evidence. We've got to figure this out. You helped figure out who destroyed the mural when you first got here, and this is so much bigger. Please."

My heart clanged inside my chest. No way my aunt hurt the mayor, but I'm not an investigator. I'm a photographer. Although my penchant for digging in to find a story qualified me as nosy. "What can I do? I did take pictures yesterday, so I can at least make a list of the people I saw. Otherwise, I'm not sure."

When my eyes met hers, the motivation to clear her name ramped inside me, but how?

Chapter Four

In the kitchen, I slipped cinnamon rolls from a can onto a baking sheet and popped them in the oven for breakfast. Scrambled eggs sizzled in my aunt's iron skillet. Though I'd never been considered the best cook, I'd learned a few tricks in my travels. I stirred the eggs for light and fluffy results. The smell of cinnamon brightened the atmosphere in the house.

Zach's hushed voice sounded through the screen door as he chatted with Aunt Cordy. I set the table with three of my aunt's Melmac plates from the 1970s. Orange, blue, and yellow flowers decorated the white background. She had kept them all these years because her momma had gifted them to her. Plus, I'm not sure a person could break one, so the entire set had survived, including the bright as sunshine yellow cups.

The rolls dripped with the gooey, white sugary substance I squeezed from the little plastic pouch. I arranged them on one of the flowered plates. Once the eggs had cooked, I called Aunt Cordy and Zach to the table. The aroma of coffee and cinnamon enticed them to join me. Zach offered a quick prayer for the food and wisdom for the day. Wisdom. If I helped Aunt Cordy try to solve the case, I'd better be loaded with wisdom.

The last time I helped with a murder, I lived in the Middle East and accidentally discovered information about someone dangerous. Turned out he had been wanted for murder. Thankfully, my co-workers and I had a local we trusted, and he helped find the man. Nightmares of his cronies chasing me through the dark streets had kept me awake for weeks. Thank goodness, I'd moved on to another town and a safer situation.

Aunt Cordy tapped my arm. "Are you going to eat?" She pointed at my plate. "Or are you lost in thought?"

"Sorry. I guess I was." I poked at the food, took a few bites, then laid my fork on the table. My aunt bit into her roll, and icing smeared her chin. She'd given years of her life to help me and Laurel whenever we needed her. I had lived with her during my junior and senior year of high school and the summers between college semesters. Laurel depended on her to help with Josephine and Henry. How could I not dig in and try to find out what happened to the mayor and who was responsible?

I sipped the coffee I had doused with almond sweet cream. Over the rim of the cup, Zach smiled at me. Not a full smile, more of an eyebrow-raised, what's-going-on smile. Had Aunt Cordy asked him to help too? I set my cup on the table. "Which vendors do you need me to call first? Do you have the list available?"

She pushed away from the table and retrieved a notepad. "This has all the names and numbers. Some of them may not answer, so be prepared to leave a message. I doubt they're aware of what happened, since the mayor was found after everyone left yesterday." She sighed and sat.

"I hadn't thought about their not knowing. Unless the local grapevine found out. Then everyone in town will have heard." I took the notepad and settled in the living room. Zach followed. "I can help make calls."

"I'll jot a few of these down and call from the porch so we aren't talking over each other." He tore a blank page out of the notepad and made quick work of writing names and numbers.

"Thanks, Zach." I watched him head outside. What a thoughtful and helpful guy. He reminded me of another man I'd known. One I had lost to nonsense.

After half an hour, Zach and Aunt Cordy and I compared notes on who we had reached. "Several of the vendors had heard the news before we called. June Bower, the mayor's ex-assistant, had spread the news." Aunt Cordy pursed her lips. "She's one to add to the suspect list."

"We don't have a list." I tapped a pencil on the notepad.

She eyed my pencil and notepad. "Let's make one."

Zach stood. "If we've reached everyone, I should go."

My aunt shook her head. "No, you don't. We need your help too."

He pushed his long dark hair behind his ear. "I haven't met many people yet or plugged myself into the community."

Before the conversation went lopsided, I stood and placed a hand on Zach's elbow and led him out the door. "You don't need to get mixed up in this if you don't want to. I'm not even sure what I'm going to do."

"Thanks. I don't want to make enemies before I get established." He ran his hand through his hair.

The compassion on his face threw me off balance. His dark eyes reminded me of... never mind. "I understand. You have the day off. Enjoy the beautiful weather." I turned and stepped onto the porch. Zach jogged across the yard as car tires crunched on the gravel drive. Laurel hopped out of her car, and her kids followed. They sprinted to the porch.

"Good morning. You in a hurry?" I stepped away from them.

Laurel told the kids to go play in the yard. "Don't go to the river." Then she pinched my t-shirt sleeve between her fingers and tugged me aside. "How's Aunt Cordy?"

I shook her off me. "She's down because we had to cancel the festival today and nervous because of the mayor's death. How did you think she'd be?" I crossed to the door and opened it. "You coming in?"

The expression on her face soured even more. She trudged behind me, and we found our aunt slumped on the couch. "Aunt Cordy?"

She startled. "I must have dozed. Didn't get much sleep last night." She rubbed her eyes. "What are you doing here?"

"I came to see you. How are you holding up? Danny wouldn't tell me anything but said I should check on you." She wrapped her arm around the older woman's shoulders.

She consoled my aunt in a way I couldn't. Laurel's compassion for people spilled out of her. I hovered in the doorway between the kitchen and living room. "Do you want something to drink?"

She waved me off. "No, I'm good. I updated the blog to reflect today's festival as a no-go. I'm sorry you can't hold your event." Laurel glanced at the clock on the mantel. "It's ten-thirty. When do people show up?"

"Thank you, dear." Aunt Cordy's gaze met Laurel's. "You can help Lyndie figure out who did this, right? I'm so afraid they'll blame me. Someone whacked him with my apple butter paddle." She wrung a handkerchief in her hands. "You girls used to work those who-dun-it puzzles when you were younger, and you played Clue all the time. I'm afraid people will stop coming to the festival if they associate it with the murder."

I knelt in front of the two of them. "Danny hasn't accused you, plus we don't have the facts on the mayor's death. Someone might have hit him with the paddle, but he may have died of another cause. I'm sure Danny will figure it out."

Laurel glared at me and spoke through her teeth. "We need to help her."

I stood and checked my watch. "Okay." I secured my aunt's notebook, and grabbed a pencil, then perched on the edge of the armchair. "Whose names should we start with on the suspect list?" In all capital letters, I wrote SUSPECTS.

"Start with June. She was angry when she lost her job." Aunt Cordy twisted a tissue in her hands.

"What about Otis?" My sister piped in.

I added his name then closed the notebook and tucked it into the crevice between the chair's arm and the cushion. "That's enough for now. I'm going to hang the closed sign on the gate." I nudged my sister's shoulder. "Want to come?" I handed her a sign Aunt Cordy had drawn while I had prepared breakfast.

"Sure. Maybe someone will have a clue as to what happened." She tied her sweater around her waist and trotted behind me. We hiked to the end of the tree-lined driveway and opened the gate. "Did you have the kids open the gate for you?"

"Henry did. He closed it too. Didn't want anyone to follow me in unexpectedly."

We opened the gate, which sat back from the road and left a space for cars to turn around, and taped the closed sign to the center. We stationed ourselves on either side of the driveway, much like my photographer cohorts and I did along the streets of the war-torn cities. My mind had reeled with memories of bombs exploding when I first arrived home, but I'd calmed and enjoyed the quiet of the homestead. I hoped the peace would remain unchanged.

Before I closed the gate, a car rumbled into the driveway, and the driver rolled her window down. "I'm sorry, the festival is closed due to unforeseen circumstances. We'll be here next weekend. Please come back." June ignored me, drove to the gate, parked, and got out of her car.

She darted at me. "It's true, isn't it?" Dark circles smudged below her eyes. Without makeup, her wrinkles deepened.

I bit my lip and waited, not wanting to reveal anything.

She craned her neck to peer into my face. "Mayor Richardson is dead."

"He is." I didn't dare say more.

Dust kicked up as a few cars slugged into the driveway. Light radiated through the scarlet and gold leaves of the maple trees and cast shadows across the drive. Dried leaves danced across the gravel in the light breeze.

Laurel spoke to a few arrivals and detoured them away. June stood in front of me and wrung her hands. "I can't believe he's gone. He was the best boss, even though he fired me." She stared into the distance.

I wrapped an arm around her shoulders. "When was the last time you spoke to the mayor?" My investigative journalism kicked in. Aunt Cordy's plea to help tugged at my heart. Did I stand beside the killer? The mayor had fired June after the mural debacle. She had paid someone to destroy the painting of the town founder. Even though she had paid to have the mural repainted and served community service, he had let her go from her job as his assistant. Today, remorse and shock painted her face, but she had also pretended innocence when she was guilty.

She shrugged away from me. "Why are you asking me when I saw him? You think I'm guilty? If you want to blame someone, talk to Marcy Fox. He refused to let her expand her business." She stomped to her car, got in, revved the engine, and then peeled out of the driveway. Laurel rushed to my side, then coughed, and waved the flying dust away with her hand. "What on earth happened? She set off a small cyclone."

"I asked when she'd last seen the mayor."

"What did she say?"

"She accused me of thinking she was guilty."

"Did you?" Laurel faced me with her hands on her hips.

I crossed my arms and glared at her. "No. I asked her when she'd last seen him. Not an accusatory question."

I stepped to the gate and shoved it closed.

"You didn't point your finger or harass her, did you?"

"Of course not."

I brushed my hands against each other to eliminate the dust. "I'm glad we were out here to see June. I'm surprised more of the townspeople didn't show to see what happened."

My sister latched the lock on the fence. "A ton of folks were at the early church service, including Danny and me. I mean, he goes when he can, but he wanted to listen for the scuttlebutt from the town people. Let me tell you, people were talking."

We hiked along the driveway to the house. "What did they say?"

She grabbed my arm and stopped me. She lowered her voice. "Had you heard Marcy Fox had argued with the mayor last week about expanding her boutique?" Her eyes widened. "I overheard her telling my neighbor all about it. She'd filed papers with his office to inquire about purchasing the small building beside her. It used to be a shoe repair store but had been empty for years. The seller wants to get rid of it, but the mayor won't give her the green light to expand on what she already has. He said the building was an eyesore and needed torn down."

"You heard a lot at church." My brain spun. "June mentioned Marcy too."

"After church in the courtyard, Danny walked to the police station and left me waiting. He wanted to check in before he took me home. The kids were playing with their friends, so I may have eavesdropped a teensy bit." She held her thumb and forefinger an inch apart.

"Let's run your *intel* past Aunt Cordy." I used air quotes. My sister's dramatic flair added spice to every conversation. As teens, she had starred in every high school play when we resided in the states, while I joined the camera club and yearbook committee.

At the house, we found our aunt on the porch staring at the blue sky. "Hey, girls. Did you send everyone away?"

"Yes, and we posted the sign in case others approach the driveway. I'm sorry you couldn't open today." I kissed her cheek. "What do you know about Marcy Fox?"

We made ourselves comfortable in the rockers. "She's been in business for about ten years. Her shop thrives in the summer. She drives a new VW Beetle and lives in a small cottage in town. She's single, and she's wrapped up in her work. The clothes and purses in her store fit the region, and she has a flair for decorating. As far as I can tell, she keeps her personal life quiet. Why?"

Laurel related the story she shared with me to our aunt. “Do you think she was angry with the mayor for blocking access to the expansion of her business? If her work is her life, she might be pretty angry.”

Aunt Cordy rubbed her nose. “She has a temper. She laid out a delivery driver for bringing the wrong packages one day when I shopped at her store. Then she called the wholesaler and let them have it, all while three customers, including me, waited on her for help.”

“Where’s the suspect list?” I stood.

My aunt took my hand and squeezed. “On the coffee table.”

I went inside to the living room and found the notebook with the names of the people we considered potential candidates for the crime and added Marcy Fox to the list. In order to take the blame off my aunt and clear the reputation of the festival, I committed to finding the killer.

Chapter Five

Monday morning, Aunt Cordy and I pinned sheets on the clothesline. The pale blue cotton fluttered in the breeze along with leaves from the maple trees. Crows cawed from the fields where they pecked at the ground. Yellow and purple chrysanthemums we had potted for the festival stood at attention along the front porch. After I fed the goats and chickens, I watered the vibrant flowers and turned the pots for full sun exposure.

Life on the homestead suited me. The peace and quiet of the early mornings reminded me of the trips I'd taken to England's Lake District. The paper I had worked for allotted me time away from the war zones in order to keep my sanity. I had traveled to Scandinavia and England any chance I got. With the weight of the mayor's murder on me, I wished I could pack my bag and head across the pond, but no. I'd help Aunt Cordy and figure this mystery out. Of course, we'd have to snoop without my brother-in-law finding out.

With all my chores finished, I drove my Jeep Cherokee Sport, one of my first purchases when I arrived home, into Seldom Seen. The man who had owned the Jeep had kept it in immaculate condition, and I adored the cherry red exterior. I passed the sign for our quaint town and pulled into a parking spot beside The Foxy Glove Boutique. Marcy Fox stood in the display window arranging cable knit sweaters and fitted flannel shirts. I scooted around to the side of the building to take a peek at the old shoe store she hoped to buy. Perhaps without the mayor around she'd move forward. Was that her plan?

Mint-green paint chipped off the aged wood siding. A crack ran down the center of the large front window, and a space gaped under the door. In the back, the exit door hung open. I placed my hand on the wooden entrance and stepped inside. The smell of vermin drove me out. Back on the sidewalk, I eyed the cement foundation. Marcy saw something I didn't. I had to find out why the mayor had left this eyesore in town and why he didn't want anyone to fix it.

I brushed a cobweb off my jacket and shoved open the boutique door. A bell tinkled overhead. An off-white counter ran along one wall with hats, leather gloves, mittens, purses, and scarves dangling from black wall racks. Mannequins wore dresses and suits, and tables, mingled throughout the store, displayed jeans and slacks. I fingered a cashmere sweater, unsure who in our little town might wear something so fancy.

Marcy climbed out of the window display. "Good morning, Lyndie."

I watched her walk towards me. Did she look guilty? I would approach this as I would any interview. Ask questions that led to other questions. "Hey, Marcy. Your store is lovely." I gestured to the dresses.

"Thank you, dear. Some things are high-end for the folks here, but we do get tourists from time to time who want something fancier." She must have caught me checking out the cashmere.

"You have a wonderful variety. Seems you're preparing for winter." I pointed to the window display.

She held her clasped hands in front of her. "I am. Want to try something on? One of the flannel shirts might be perfect for life on the farm."

I swear she blushed and turned on her southern charm.

She lifted a lightweight winter coat from a rack on the wall. "This arrived yesterday. It has a lining that zips in and out depending on the temperature. Of course, we don't freeze like our northern neighbors, but we do get a nip in the air."

"I remember. I'm anticipating less outdoor work this winter. Aunt Cordy has taught me about orchard upkeep all summer." I laughed.

She hooked the hanger back on the rack. In a lowered voice, she asked the question I had anticipated. "Is it true?"

I bit my lower lip and waited.

She stepped closer to me. "I heard the mayor died Saturday night." A pained expression wrinkled her forehead.

I nodded. "It's true."

She shook her head, and her bleached blond curls swung from side to side. "Such a shame."

"It truly is." I patted her arm. "What time did you pack and leave Saturday? Lots of people stopped by your booth." Okay, question number one asked.

She crossed her arms. "Oh, my yes, I had so many ladies stop and ask what I was adding to the store for fall and winter. Of course I had several items with me, and I was prepared to ask May Joy to bring more if I needed, but she called me and asked me to come back before four. I skedaddled out of there."

Did she go back to the store or to the river?

"I talked to him at the festival, and now I can't believe he's gone. We had a bit of a rift. I want so much to buy the building behind me, and he said no to my business plan." She slapped a hand over her mouth.

"You and the mayor had a disagreement?"

She shoved her hair away from her face, then flipped her hand in the air. "Nothing much. More differing opinions. I begged to turn the building into additional retail space, and he argued the old thing should be torn down."

"How desperate were you to get your hands on it? It's falling down and kind of small." I placed myself between her and the door, in case I needed to run. Dramatic, but I had to protect myself in case I spooked her.

She placed a hand on each hip, and her skirt, printed with autumn leaves, swished. "I'm not desperate." Her voice rose an octave. "I'd never harm the mayor to get an old building." She turned and tromped behind the counter. "If you aren't here to buy something, you can leave."

Before she threw something at me, I turned and exited the building. Marcy protested too much. She'd left the festival early for a supposed store emergency. How much of an emergency could a boutique suffer? She might not have intended harm, but she could have followed Mayor Richardson to the river to talk. She may have taken Aunt Cordy's paddle with her for protection. The apple butter paddle had leaned against the table in plain sight, in my aunt's booth. What if she feared he might hurt her? I'd share my speculations with Aunt Cordy and Laurel.

*****

Later in the afternoon, gravel crunched under my tires as I wound along the driveway to Aunt Cordy's house, my home. Wispy clouds floated across the brightest blue sky. We couldn't complain about October's weather. Walt had parked his truck with a small animal trailer near the barn, and he and my aunt huddled near it. A soft bleat I didn't recognize cried from the trailer. It didn't sound like our goats. Somehow the quiet baa sounded happy.

I parked the Jeep next to them and climbed out of my car. I bit back the urge to spill my visit with Marcy. "Hey, Walt. Good to see you." He dropped Aunt Cordy's hand and waved to me.

"Good to see you too. Your aunt and I were talking about you." He patted her shoulder.

Wonder why they were talking about me? "What's going on?" A bleat echoed in the trailer. "What have you got in there?" I took a step to the end of the metal encasement.

Walt leaned in front of me and blocked my view. "I have a gift for you. My friend Jonesy is retiring from farming and moving to Florida. He sold his cattle and most of his sheep, but these two are special. Meant for someone to love and have as pets."

He opened the gate on the back of the trailer and led out the most beautiful creatures I'd ever met, and I'd seen many animals in my travels. Black eyes, set in sweet, round fuzzy black faces, blinked at me. Short, twisted horns grew from their heads, and black ears stuck out. Long white curls draped across their bodies, and their little black knees made me smile. Darling was the only word in my brain. "What kind of sheep are they?"

A grin spread across Walt's face. "They are Valais Blacknose sheep. Two ewes."

"Wait. I read they lived in Switzerland and didn't come to the US." I petted one of the sheep's fleece. "She's so soft. I've heard of the breed, and I'm surprised to see them here."

He handed me the tethered ropes. "They are in Switzerland, but a few other countries have been able to acquire them. New Zealand has a program where a breeder can purchase an embryo and breed his or her own sheep. Jonesy did, and his ewe produced these beautiful twins. He'd wanted one for years, ever since he visited a farm in North Carolina who raises them. Cost him a pretty penny, but he loved on these girls for three years now. He couldn't bear to sell them, so I told him I had someone in mind who would appreciate them. With all your travels and travails, I hoped you might enjoy these two, and they will bring you comfort."

Walt knew about the man who had died in my arms in the Middle East. My best friend, Elias, who I had planned to marry, got caught in a crossfire as we shot photos. My heart ripped in two, and three months later I left my job and traveled home. I knelt beside these gorgeous girls and stopped short of nuzzling my face into their fleece. "Do they have names?"

"Jonesy called this one Thimble, and her sister is Floss. His wife had been a seamstress before she passed, and he wanted to honor her. These two brought him a lot of comfort after Bess passed. He even let them into the house from time to time. I'm not sure Bess would have let him." Walt chuckled. "What do you think? Want to keep them?"

"Yes. If it's okay with you, Aunt Cordy?" I rose from the ground. "Do we have a place for them?"

My aunt nodded. "We have the little shed near the barn with two sides and a shared center. It's right by the field where they can graze. I think the goats will enjoy them too. Maybe they'll keep Happy and Bashful out of trouble. Plus, we have Murphy for protection." She petted the sheep. "They're both beautiful, and Jonesy gave them baths before he left."

"He did. He said he bathed them at least once a month and sheared them twice a year. Their fleece grows twice as fast as most sheep, and the coat comes off in one piece." Walt's face shone with pride in his friend. "I'm gonna miss him. We played cards every Friday night with our buddies. We'll have to find another fella." He nudged my aunt.

“Not me. I’m not hanging around with a bunch of old fogies. How about you get some young blood in the game?”

Zach sauntered into the barnyard. “Zach would be the perfect addition.” Aunt Cordy pointed to the young man. “He’s forty-something. Perfect to round out you old guys.”

Walt shook his head. “I’m barely over sixty, Cordelia.”

I laughed at their banter. “He means business when he uses your real name.”

Zach’s gaze moved to each of us, and a question formed in his eyes. His brow wrinkled, then a smile split his face. “What’s going on, and who are these two?” He knelt beside Thimble.

I knelt on the other side of her. “She’s a Valais Blacknose sheep Walt gifted to me, and this is her sister, Floss. Aren’t they lovely?” We rose to stand.

“They are.”

“Let’s get them settled.” Aunt Cordy wasted no time. “They can graze in the pasture while you prepare the shed. There’s straw in the barn.”

I led Floss and Thimble to the gate, and Zach drew it open. The two stepped in, and I removed the ropes. The bells around their necks jingled. “Jonesy had added the bells so he could keep track of where they roamed.” Walt stepped into the field behind us with my aunt at his side. He latched the gate then unloaded a bag of feed by the barn.

“Here come Bashful and Happy. I hope the goats are kind to Floss and Thimble.” A protective instinct welled up in me.

"They are sniffing them." Once they finished inspection, they bounded across the field, and the sheep nibbled on grass.

"I'm glad you like them, Lyndie. They'll be perfect pets."

I side-hugged Walt. "Thank you for thinking of me. They're delightful." Walt tapped Zach on the shoulder. "Young man, do you play cards?"

I wandered to the small shed to prepare a home for Floss and Thimble and let the gentlemen discuss playing cards. The tin roof on the shed stood a few inches above my head. I opened the low door and bent over to step inside. Aunt Cordy and I had cleaned it a while back since the goats lived in the barn and no other animals had occupied it all summer. A small wooden bench sat along one wall which I could move outside if I wanted to visit with my girls. I swept away cobwebs from the ceiling and dirt from the floor with the broom I'd grabbed from the barn. I hoped I hadn't disturbed Charlotte or her web. I returned the broom, then gathered straw and loaded it into the wheelbarrow. Back in the shed, I spread it on the floor, then I added a water bottle and a metal feeder. I shaped the girls' new home into a warm, comforting place, and a spot where I'd decompress and relax. Walt and Jonesy understood loss and sensed I needed someone, even sheep, to talk to and cuddle. Yes, Floss and Thimble offered something I no longer had. An ear to listen who wanted nothing in return. Elias had listened to my ongoing conversations and never expected anything. He had treated me as a princess and a partner, even in my dungarees and t-shirts. A fellow photographer and journalist, he taught me patience. His French upbringing had shown me how to slow down and wait. My heart ached yet I thanked the Lord for my time with him. As the shroud of sorrow around my heart eased, I longed to find purpose again.

Thimble nudged my leg, and I wrapped my arms around her neck. "I already love you, girl."

My sadness of losing Elias reminded me of the poor mayor. Had anyone loved the mayor? Did he have someone to hug?

While I figured out the rest of my life, I'd focus on who killed Mayor Richardson. As much as I appreciated the quiet life on the farm, I missed ferreting out and reporting truth.

Chapter Six

With the sheep settled in the pasture, I trekked to the house. Laurel's car had taken the place of Walt's truck and trailer in the driveway. Laughter drifted through the afternoon air, and my stomach growled. In my excitement for my new buddies, I'd forgotten to eat lunch. Zach, Aunt Cordy, and Laurel rocked on the porch in the rockers. My aunt had added four of them in her favorite shade of red a few years ago. I'm not sure if she loved the color because of her shiny red apples or if she'd embraced the color since childhood. Either way, she spread the shades of scarlet around her homestead.

I skipped up the steps. "Laurel, you have to see my new pets."

Zach handed me a glass of iced tea. "Thank you." I took a gulp and then sat in a chair beside my sister.

Laurel stared at me.

"What? Do I have something on my nose?" I swiped my hand across my face.

"No." She rested her hand on mine. "Were you in town this morning?"

In my excitement over the sheep, I'd forgotten about my conversation with Marcy Fox. The chat I had with her had stretched behind me like it had happened a week ago. "Yes. I dropped by the Foxy Glove." I snatched a cookie from the plate on the side table to calm my grumbling stomach.

"What did she say?" Laurel perched on the edge of her chair, legs crossed.

I would have rather talked about my new sheep, but I promised Aunt Cordy I'd see this through, and Laurel wanted information now. I loved my sister, but sometimes she pushed me too far. Most would expect I'd be the bossy one, as the eldest, but no. Laurel won the prize for that. Even as kids, she tried to direct what we played. If we pretended to play school, she was always the teacher. One time she played the part of principal, and I had to go to her pretend office and admit I chewed gum in class. I didn't even chew gum as a kid.

I bit off another piece of cookie, then sipped my tea. "Marcy says she left the festival at four o'clock due to a store emergency. Which means she may have left her booth and followed the mayor to the river. If he was going for a walk, she may have seen an opportunity to argue with him about the building she wanted to purchase. He had shot her down before, so I think she wanted to try her charm on him and ask again. What if she took the apple butter paddle from your booth?" I glanced at Aunt Cordy. "I'm not taking her off the list yet, but I gotta tell you, the building she wants smells like mice and is falling down."

Laurel stood and paced, then stopped in front of me. "How did she react to you?"

"She told me to get out of her store. Maybe she figured out my angle and thought I'd accused her of killing the mayor." I finished my tea. "Her little store has some high-end fashion. Fancy for Seldom Seen, although she said she gets tourists who want cashmere."

"Marcy is kind of uppity, which is funny since she grew up here. I heard she bragged about the car her parents bought her in high school, then she worked two jobs after school to pay for it. Plus, she lived in a smaller house than this one." My sister pointed at the front door, then leaned on the porch railing. "All according to town grapevine."

Laurel tugged on her ear. "I overheard Danny on the phone last night but couldn't understand all of the conversation. He walked to the kitchen, and I sat in the living room with the television on. The kids were watching a movie."

My impatience bubbled inside me and competed with my grumbling tummy. "What did you hear?"

She gave me one of the let-me-tell-my-story glares. "The only name I made out was Johnson. Could be Johnson Winters or Ross Johnson or one of his brothers. Do you know anything about Johnson Winters? He's only lived here a short time."

Zach cleared his throat. "I spoke to him at the festival. He told me he's been doing odd jobs around town, but he has a background in conservation, and he asked if I'd heard of any jobs in the area. Being new myself, I gave him a website to check but told him I didn't have any contacts."

Aunt Cordy stopped her rocker. "What time did you talk to him?"

Zach eyed the porch ceiling, then turned to my aunt. "Between three-thirty and four, I think."

"So, he was on the premises about the time Danny estimated the mayor died." Aunt Cordy took to rocking again.

Now, I paced the porch. "What motive would he have? He's lived here for a few months. Were Ross Johnson or any of his brothers at the festival?"

Zach shrugged. "I have no idea."

Laurel regarded our aunt. "Did you see any of them? Roland stopped at my booth to ask me to put an ad on the website for him. He's selling one of his trucks, but I didn't see Ross or Rob."

Our aunt shook her head and pursed her lips. A shadow of despair crossed her face. No doubt thinking about the finger Danny pointed at her.

Silence filled the air until my sister spoke. "What were you saying about pets or sheep or something?"

Relief coursed through me. When we discussed the mayor's demise, my heart beat too fast and my palms sweat. The weight of solving a mystery sent spikes of fear through me, even as I wanted to help solve this and get my aunt off the hook. The therapy my former employer forced me to take when I returned home proved I didn't suffer from PTSD, even though I'd experienced the horrors of war. She found, however, that I had developed anxiety. Loud noises and chaotic environments gave me headaches and tensed my body. The medication she prescribed helped, along with my quiet time with God. The book of Psalms often eased my fear and distress. Even still, I had to stay vigilant. Those two beautiful sheep fit in with my need for peace.

I took my sister's hand. "Follow me." At the fence, I stopped and tugged on the metal gate. My sister stepped in with me, and then I secured it so my precious new friends couldn't escape. Happy and Bashful stood on the weathered wooden spools my aunt had procured from the electric company. They contented themselves with jumping on and off the platforms. Aunt Cordy had painted the spools yellowish-green and bluish-purple because she'd read goats see those colors best. Out beside the shed, my fluffy pets grazed. I pointed to them. "There they are."

"Oh, my goodness, they're adorable." She sprinted across the field, and I followed. "I've never seen sheep like them. Their faces are so cute."

I explained how Walt and Jonesy gifted them to me. "This one is Floss, and her sister is Thimble."

She ran her hand through Floss's fleece, and Floss baaed in return. "How do you tell them apart?"

I petted Thimble. "This one is a hair bigger, and her collar is pink. Floss's collar is teal. Aren't they the sweetest?" I snuggled between them and hugged their necks.

Laurel ran a hand over Floss's head. "They have the perfect names for you. Don't you use a thimble and floss when you embroider those fancy patterns you learned overseas?"

I moved to stand beside my sister. "I hadn't thought of my embroidery, but you're right. Now, I want to make sheep ornaments in the Scandinavian style. Like they do the horses. With flowers, leaves, and fancy loops. I might sell them at the festival next year. Or give them as gifts." I'd purchase wool fabric and floss from Jonquil's shop, Baa Baa Black Sheep. She sold all kinds of fiber craft materials. She might want to buy the fleece from me when I sheared the sheep, or I might barter for supplies.

We each patted the sheep and then hiked back to the gate. Laurel unhitched the latch. "I can't wait for Josephine and Henry to see them. Can I bring them after school?" She pulled her phone from her pocket and checked the time. "I have to go pick them up. We'll run by after dinner." She darted to her car, and I ambled to the house. A happy glow emanated from my insides out. A few minutes with my buddies lightened my anxiety.

Aunt Cordy had left Zach on the porch. I joined him in one of the rockers, and the information I had learned about someone named Johnson churned in my head and disrupted my pleasant relaxation with the sheep. Zach stared at the barn. "Any important clues in there?"

He turned and stared at me. "I want to help find who killed the mayor."

His words startled me. Why would a new-to-town guy want to help? So, I asked. "Why?"

He pushed his long bangs behind his ears, and his brown eyes focused on my face. He rubbed the beard on his chin. "I was accused of something I didn't do before I moved to Seldom Seen. My cousin had convinced me to put in an application for the job I have now. After I did I about lost my chance." He sipped his watered-down tea. "Someone had robbed the lighthouse keeper's cottage the night I sat at the lighthouse praying about my decision whether to move or not. The police blamed me. Wrong place, wrong time. The police leaned on me as the prime suspect, even though I had never done anything against the law. I was a naturalist and park ranger for crying out loud. Why would I jeopardize the job I'd had for close to twenty years? Thankfully, a friend and I discovered who stole the money." He sighed. "Not really a happy ending, but at least I was proven innocent. Which motivates me to put the person who did this behind bars. Plus, there is no way your aunt is guilty. She's one of the kindest humans I've met."

My heart hurt for Zach. To be accused of something you didn't do, then having to find the thief yourself took guts. I wanted him on our side. Between Laurel, our aunt, Zach and me, we'd find the mayor's killer and the reason behind his death. In the meantime, I'd enjoy Floss and Thimble. "We'd love to have your help. Of course, Danny and the police are searching for the suspect, but I want to clear Aunt Cordy's name and get the person off the streets. The last thing we need is a killer running around. Besides, snooping gives me something to do besides farm work."

"Makes sense."

Zach had spent almost twenty years in his last job, so why leave? "Did you grow up on Lake Erie?" Why else would he stay in the same place for so long unless he'd been married or something?

He crossed his ankles. "I grew up near Cincinnati and attended a small private college after public school. My sister and I vacationed in Marblehead and on the islands with our parents. She moved to Scotland after college to study weaving, I miss her." He uncrossed his legs and leaned forward. "In college, I interned with the Ohio Department of Resources on the lake and landed my job after graduation. Once there, I never left. I spent years building the education programs, but after twenty years I wanted something new. Since not too many ladies want to spend time with nerdy guys, I seldom date. I'd hoped a change of scenery might put some life in my, well, my life." He grinned.

I couldn't hold back a giggle. "You'd be surprised how many of us females appreciate guys like you. I'm glad you're here, and I hope we can figure out this mystery together."

Chapter Seven

Rain drizzled from low-hanging gray clouds on Tuesday morning, with no promise of stopping soon. In my flowered mud boots and emerald slicker, I carried hay to the shed for Floss and Thimble. Our silly goats, Bashful and Happy, trounced through puddles and splashed each other. Murphy ran his patrol along the fenceline. Inside the shed, I poured the feed into the trough and dropped onto the bench. My mornings brightened when I spent time sitting with my new buddies. Their presence brought me a sense of peace, plus they listened and never talked back, except for the occasional baa.

"Morning, girls." They nibbled on the hay. "You two must be warm in your woolly coats." I ran my fingers through Thimble's fleece. "I don't suppose you have answers to the mystery."

Floss nudged my hand. "Hey, girl. I love your round face and those dark eyes. Did you have fun with Josephine and Henry last night? They sure loved you." I gave the girls a final pat.

Aunt Cordy mentioned at breakfast the door on the barn needed to be fixed. The rail hook had come loose, and the door sagged to one side. Without our sliding door, the goats might escape and cause havoc in the yard. On my way to the house, I tested the lopsided door and it jammed. Sounded like a reason to call Johnson Winters, one of our suspects.

In the house, I went in search of my aunt. I found her in the den at her desk, with her head bent over a ledger. "Can I interrupt you a minute?"

Her gaze peered over her reading glasses. "Sure, what's going on?"

I settled into my aunt's vintage tub chair, a putrid green seat with round arms made before I was born. Many times, I'd witnessed Aunt Cordy in the chair reading, with her feet on a mismatched ottoman. Its stuffing contoured to fit my aunt and snugged me if I scooted in far enough. Aside from the color, the old thing appealed to me. "What do you think about asking Johnson Winters to fix the door on the barn? The rail the rollers hang from is falling, and every time I open it, I think it's going to drop on my head."

She folded her hands in her lap. "I don't want either of us to get hurt. Call him. I have his contact information from when he fixed the hole in the barn roof." Her teeth showed when she smiled. "You want to interrogate him while he's here, don't you?"

I picked at my fingernails, then raised my head to face my aunt. "Let's not call it interrogation. I might ask a few questions or simply observe. We do want to solve the mystery. Right?"

"We do. Be careful, please." Her eyes pleaded as she spoke. "As much as I want to know what happened, I don't want another body down."

Me neither. The last thing I wanted was for harm to fall on any of us, or anyone in town. "I promise I'll be careful."

Within an hour, I dialed my phone from the kitchen.

Mr. Winters picked up on the third ring. "Winter's, I'll fix what you don't want to."

Interesting greeting. "Hi. Johnson Winters?" Of course he answered the phone, so why ask if it was him? A herd of cows stomped around in my stomach as I tried to act calm and together. You'd think after all I'd witnessed and faced in my photojournalist job, I'd stay calm.

"Sure is. How can I help you?"

He sounded friendly. "This is Lyndie Lavender. My aunt and I have a barn door in need of repair. Are you available to check it out and fix it?" I waited.

"Let me check my schedule." The sound of papers shuffling whispered through the phone. "I can come by Thursday morning about ten. Didn't I fix your barn roof a while back? You're the place with the apple festival, right? Where the mayor died?"

Surprised he connected my name with the festival and mentioned the mayor, I quieted. What if he suspected that we suspected him?

"Yes, we live on the homestead where my aunt hosts the apple festival. The festival opens again on Saturday." Not certain why I added that piece of information, I waited for his reply.

"If the job isn't too big, I might get it fixed Thursday or Friday."

"I'll see you Thursday morning." I clicked off the phone and hurried to Aunt Cordy's den. "He's coming Thursday morning. He said he might have time to fix it then or on Friday. I'd love to have it finished before Saturday. And he mentioned the mayor."

She pulled her glasses off her face. "Oh. Did he seem hesitant?"

I lounged in her chair again. "Not at all. He knew who we were and where to come. What if he'd scoped out the place before the mayor died? He may have made himself familiar with our farm, so he had an idea of where to lure the mayor."

My aunt raised her hand to stop me. "Hold on. Your imagination is in overdrive. How about we see how he acts when he's here?"

"Will do." Of course, she was right.

Aunt Cordy rubbed the bridge of her nose. "I've been meaning to ask. Have you gone through the photos you took at the festival on Saturday? Something might jump out at you."

Every minute of the past few days had been filled with anything but photo browsing, and I'd meant to share photos with Danny. "I'm going to look at them now. Thanks for reminding me." I hustled from the den, up the stairs, and into my room.

Seated on the bed, I plugged the card reader into my laptop and pushed the SD card in. A file opened with the pictures I had taken on Saturday. Aunt Cordy stood inside her booth holding jars of apple butter. Her smile gleamed. In the background, her apple butter paddles lined up on the table. The biggest one rested on the edge near the tent's exit. The timestamp on the photo read ten fifteen in the morning. A photo of her and Walt followed, and a few of Josephine and Henry with the animals. Roland and Rob Johnson stood at the pens with their children. The littlest boy, with wispy blond hair, patted the nose of Bashful the goat. Laurel had overheard the name Johnson, but surely a dad with children in tow wouldn't harm someone the day he took his little ones to the festival.

I flipped through several before I spotted Johnson Winters chatting with Marcy Fox. Interesting. Perhaps two people had joined forces. What if Marcy had promised Johnson the job to refurbish the broken-down building she wanted to expand into, but the mayor's refusal cost him the job? He'd make good money on such a big job. What if he and Marcy were an item, and he wanted to help her achieve her dream? What if none of this were true?

I moved on to photos snapped later in the day. A man I didn't recognize appeared in the background of several photos. In every one of them, he watched the mayor. Who was he? Why did he follow Mayor Richardson to every booth? He wore a fedora and a long raincoat on a day with no rain. I was surprised I hadn't noticed him the day of the festival, but I'd been busy. Aunt Cordy might recognize him. In the next photo, Ross Johnson chatted with Jonquil at the Baa Baa Black Sheep booth. With both hands on the table, he leaned close to her and smiled. The only thing I'd accuse him of was having a crush on our local weaver.

I unplugged my laptop and carried it downstairs. Still in her den, I interrupted my aunt one more time. "I want to show you a few photos of a guy I don't recognize. He appears to be shadowing the mayor in several photos?"

Aunt Cordy positioned the laptop on her desk, and I sat in a wooden folding chair beside her. "See." I clicked through three photos. "He's following Mayor Richardson in every photo. Who is he?"

She studied the photos. "I've never seen him before."

"Me neither. He's not dressed like any of the other festivalgoers." I clicked through two more pictures. "In this one, his coat is off. I can't tell how old he is, but he has a rather prominent nose, not to mention a tan."

"Laurel might recognize him." She tapped on the screen. "She's bringing the kids by after school to help me bake cookies."

"That's a good activity on this rainy day." I lifted my laptop from the desk. "I'm going to send Danny some photos. He might have met the mystery guy."

At four o'clock, Laurel and the kids rolled into the driveway. The rain had stopped but left a chill in the air. I watched Josephine and Henry tromp across the barnyard and into the field to see Floss and Thimble. They petted the sheep as the goats danced around them.

Laurel called after them. "Kids, when you come in the house, leave your boots on the porch."

I hooked my arm into hers and led her to the house. We found our aunt in the kitchen preparing dough for cut-out cookies. She had made them with us when we were young. The almond flavoring she added gave them a deliciousness I'd not tasted anywhere else. Probably because they tasted like home.

My sister hugged her. "Smells wonderful in here. I love your special cookies. What shapes are you making today?"

Aunt Cordy dusted confectioner's sugar from her hands. She rolled out the dough on a sugared surface instead of a floured one. "Leaves and apples. I'm going to offer them to the folks who visit my booth. Of course, I'll make sure I have some on hand in here for you girls and the kiddos."

Josephine and Henry bounded into the kitchen. "We're ready to make cookies."

"Not until you wash your hands. You were out with the animals." Laurel waved them to the sink.

"We know, Mom." Their response sounded as if they'd practiced.

While Aunt Cordy and the kids rolled and cut dough, Laurel and I escaped to the living room. The same furniture our aunt chose for the room thirty years ago still filled it. When she had married Uncle Wes, she had left behind her desire for a magazine-worthy home and fancy clothes for a simple life in the foothills of Appalachia. The familiarity of the floral border on the pale pink pinstripe walls wrapped me in a hug. She had kept our pink and teal beanbag chairs and the classic record player we'd listened to her old records on.

Laurel and I huddled on the navy-blue plaid couch with the laptop. "I want you to look through these with me." I called up the file and clicked the first photo.

She pointed to the one of Johnson Winters and Marcy. "Huh. They're cozy."

"Do you suppose they're in cahoots?" Winters frowned at Marcy in one and smiled in the next. She stood eye-level with him in the frown photo, then sat when he smiled. Then, her mouth turned down and shoulders slumped in the next one. "Maybe he's in line to repair the building next to hers, if she got approved to use it."

We moved through the photos to the fellow with the raincoat and fedora. "Any idea who this guy is?" I pointed at him in a few of the photos, then in the ones where he had removed his coat.

"His name is Greg Garrison. I met him at Delight's bakery the other morning. He appears to keep to himself. I'm surprised to see him at the Apple Fest." She scrunched her forehead. "Did you send any photos to Danny?"

"Yes. About an hour ago. I'd been so busy, I hadn't sorted through them yet." We stared at the mystery man. "Something about him reminds me of a man I met in Scotland. He followed me into a shop and questioned me about my photos. I found out he worked for a rival magazine that wanted me to work for them. Except he was much younger."

"Did you get many offers to work for other magazines and newspapers?" She cocked her head to one side.

"On occasion, but not often. He had read my article on the women in Afghanistan who ran their own businesses. You'd be surprised what difficulties they had to fight through to make their mark. My heart went out to them, so I wanted to feature them in an article."

"I read what you wrote and appreciated the photos you featured. Life must be so difficult for them." Laurel sighed. "If they can get through the obstacles they face, we can help figure out who killed the mayor."

"Good point. By the way, Johnson Winters is coming in the morning to estimate the repair of the barn door. I'm hoping he can fix it, plus I want to ask a few questions."

"Good luck, sister."

"Thanks, I'll need it."

Chapter Eight

The gray clouds lingered in Wednesday's dreary sky. The light mist and hidden sun suited the day of the mayor's funeral. On television, law enforcement and amateur sleuths attended the funeral of the victim to watch the people, aka suspects, but today, I wanted to honor the man whose efforts improved our small town, instead of spy on others. Although I'd keep my eyes on anyone named Johnson and the man in the fedora, if he showed.

I joined my aunt in the kitchen. Dressed in black slacks and a maroon top, she gathered containers from the refrigerator and placed them in a plastic laundry basket, along with a jug of tea. "I'll carry the crock-pot." I unplugged it and snugged it into the carrier pouch to keep it warm.

"Thanks, dear." She turned to me. Her eyes watered. "Such a sad day. Danny searched for members of the mayor's family but found no one. The funeral director arranged everything with the help of Pastor Clements and the mayor's new assistant, Becky. At least we can provide a meal for the town folks who come."

"I'm guessing several residents will attend. Laurel told me many of the shops are closing at noon so they can come." I opened the door, and she carried the basket to the Jeep while I locked the house.

We loaded the food and settled in for the drive to the church.

"I'm glad they're having the service at the church." My aunt flipped the mirror down on the visor and checked her hair.

"Me too." A few minutes later, I parked in the back lot by the fellowship hall. We unloaded the food and carried it into the kitchen.

A few ladies from my aunt's Sunday school class took the basket and crock-pot and shooed us to the sanctuary for the visitation and service, while they prepared arrangements for the meal.

A crowd snaked around the sanctuary as they waited to share their sympathy, even though the pastor and his wife were the only ones receiving people. Until June arrived. The woman hustled through the crowd and parked herself beside the closed casket. She stared at the crowd, then flung herself across the top of the casket and wailed. The commotion she caused knocked the mayor's photo off the table and the flower spray of carnations, tinted in the shades of autumn, onto the floor.

The pastor's wife, Sally, patted June's back and with a gentle touch pulled her away from the coffin and led her to a seat. The pastor restored order to the front of the sanctuary, and folks continued to move around the room.

June wailed louder than the piped-in music. My heart ached for her. She had cared about her former employer, but could she have smacked him on the head? I shook away the picture in my head of her swinging the paddle.

Danny, Laurel, and Officer Ashton stood stationed along the wall near the front doors of the church. Danny and Officer Ashton, dressed in official uniforms, perused the crowd. Did they think the killer came to view his prey? Laurel kissed her hubby on the cheek, then strode toward Aunt Cordy and me. She hugged our aunt, then leaned into me. "Anyone look suspicious to you?"

I arched my eyebrows. "Not yet. I'm trying to honor the mayor. Not find the murderer." I shrugged my shoulders.

She scooted a smidge closer to me. "I think Danny and Officer Ashton are hoping to find a clue. He didn't tell me he was here to search out suspects, but that's what they do on television shows and movies. Right?"

"I suppose." Hadn't I thought the same? "They may be paying their respects, but either way, I'm going to go through the line and pay mine." As soon as the words left my mouth, Marcy Fox and Johnson Winters stepped through the door. Marcy wore a black, below the knee sheath. The bodice of black lace over gold lame peeked from under her black fur stole. Fancy, for a funeral. I had noticed the stole at the Foxy Glove last week. She either bought one for herself or she'd hang the one she wore back in the window and perhaps add a discount tag. I preferred my black skirt and simple black and pink top with flats.

Johnson Winters, the antithesis of Marcy, sported dark jeans and a tucked in, button down. She clung to his arm and teetered in her three-inch heels and dabbed her eyes with a handkerchief.

She must have cared more about the mayor than we knew. Or she was involved in his death. What if they'd dated, and he dumped her? Nope, not going there today. I'd tuck away the idea for tomorrow.

Aunt Cordy, Laurel, and I reached the front of the church. We each shook Pastor Clements' hand and spoke words of condolence. The odor of carnations and roses reminded me of my grandmother's funeral. Something about the flowers meant for comfort induced my gag reflex. The photo of the mayor stared at us from the table June had knocked into. A wide grin crossed his face. The idea of his death left me questioning my own life. Why had Elias died and not me? I stood in the line of fire as much as he did. My heart ached for him and for the folks who missed the mayor.

Pastor Clements delivered a powerful message about living life to the fullest, like the mayor had. If nothing else, I'd leave the service today with the desire to allow God to lead me to new opportunities. I'd hidden on my aunt's homestead for six months. The Lord had heard my cries to open myself to life again.

As we filed out of the sanctuary to the cemetery next to the church, I caught sight of the man in the fedora. He clung to the outskirts of the crowd. As soon as the pastor spoke his final words, the man disappeared. His distance from the funeral attendees appeared suspicious, or he wanted to show respect without joining the rest of us. How did Danny track down criminals day in and day out? Of course, Seldom Seen's crime scene remained minimal most of the time, but still, the constant awareness daunted me.

After the funeral, many of the mourners gathered in the fellowship hall. I have never understood why we eat after we lay someone in the ground. The nature of our funeral customs had puzzled me for years. I appreciate a good meal as much as anyone, but after Elias had died, I longed to be alone with my thoughts, alone with God, to sit outdoors beside a stream or lake, but my friends insisted on taking me to eat at a local eatery after the small ceremony they arranged for me.

I reached into my pocket and pulled out the leather heart he had a local artist in Turkey make for me. The leather artist had engraved a floral and feather pattern into the leather and attached it to a small metal circle. I had hooked it onto a bracelet and worn it until I almost lost it. That day, I moved the beautiful treasure to my pocket or purse. I had carried the symbol of love with me ever since.

"Lyndie, are you going to eat your pie?" Laurel nudged me with her elbow.

I poked my fork into an apple and a bite of crust. "Yes. I never pass up Aunt Cordy's pie." As I spoke, I eyed Otis. He grinned, and his voice sounded across the room.

"The mayor and I didn't see things the same, but we planned to work together when I took office. The election is a ways off, but I hope I have your vote." He patted his chest.

I turned my head to Laurel. "What is he doing? This isn't the place for campaigning." Before I stopped myself, I stood and stalked across the room.

"Otis, can I speak to you?" My temples throbbed.

He stood and faced me. "Whatever you want to say, you can say here."

"Fine." I placed a hand on my hip and pointed a finger at his face. "This is not the place or time to ask for votes. We are here to honor the man who ran our town. Whether you cared for him or not, you need to show some respect." I turned and walked outside. The cemetery called to me, and I followed. I found the cement bench installed at the entrance for folks to sit near their loved ones.

Footsteps echoed on the pavement behind me. Laurel lowered herself beside me on the bench, which overlooked the graves. She sat next to me and stared ahead. "What happened in there?"

I wiped my hand across my eyes and snuffled. "My anger."

"Over the mayor?" Her voice rose.

I rested my head in my hands. "No. Over the unfairness of life."

My sister handed me a tissue. "This is about Elias?"

I blew my nose, then stared at the headstones. "Yes. I loved him more than I believed possible. He was the kindest man I'd ever met, and he cared about me. He watched out for me, and I never told you—he saved my life. If he hadn't jumped in front of me, I would have died. Instead, he's gone." More tears poured down my cheeks.

Laurel placed a hand on my back. "I'm so sorry." The tears in her voice touched my heart. My beautiful sister cried with me. We sat in the quiet for a while.

The sound of cars starting and muffled voices pulled me out of my daze, and my sister too.

She rose from the bench. "Want me to take you home?"

"What about Aunt Cordy?" I sniffed.

"I'll tell her what's going on. She can drive herself home." Laurel took my keys and hurried into the church then returned after a few minutes. "All set. She said she'd see you in a bit."

We loaded into the car, and I rode home in silence. At the house, I hugged Laurel, then stepped back. She placed a hand on each of my shoulders. "Thanks for telling me what happened. I didn't want to ask, but I hoped you'd share when you were ready. I sensed you had loved him, and I'm so sorry for your hurting heart." She patted my arm and left.

In the house, the quiet caused an ache in my soul. I hustled upstairs and changed into jeans and a sweatshirt. After I tied my gym shoes, I hiked into the field where my sheep skipped to me. Seeing their cheery faces lifted a burden I'd carried for months. Once I had shared the truth with Laurel, the heaviness in my heart lightened. I hadn't faced the truth until today. Elias had given his life for mine, the ultimate sacrifice.

In my distress and grief, I clung to the twenty-third Psalm. My shepherd's goodness and love followed me. Even as I tried to catch a killer.

Chapter Nine

Thursday morning, low-hanging clouds floated toward the next county, and dewdrops sparkled in the field. Floss and Thimble grazed in the meadow on broadleaf plantain and chicory, as I snapped photos of my beauties. The mountains made a gorgeous background of gold, scarlet, and orange, with smatterings of spruce green. I breathed in the early morning mountain air. A few moments in God's creation filled my soul with peace.

In the house, I snatched a couple of the cookies Josephine and Henry had baked. The sweet almond flavor melted on my tongue. My coffee balanced the taste of sugar with much-needed caffeine. I settled at the table, and Aunt Cordy shuffled into the room. "Good morning."

She kissed me on the forehead. "Morning. How did you sleep?"

"Not great, but enough." I sipped more coffee. "Took my coffee black this morning, so I didn't feel guilty about eating cookies for breakfast."

My aunt threw her head back, and her laughter rang through the kitchen. I loved it when she let loose. Her sense of humor had helped my sister and me when we missed our parents.

"Any plans today?" She poured herself a cup of coffee. Jeans and a sweatshirt didn't hide my aunt's healthy beauty.

"A little before ten, I'm going to sit on the porch and wait for Mr. Winters. I plan to hang around while he checks the door." At the sink, I rinsed my cup, then set it on the counter. "Save me some coffee for later."

At nine forty-five, I planted myself on the porch with Murphy at my feet. Aunt Cordy joined me with an enamel pan, a paper bag filled with her Golden Delicious apples, and her paring knife. She held the apple in one hand and trimmed off the skin in one long curly tail. I'd attempted this feat many times and failed on every one. After years of peeling apples, she'd earned the gift.

"You amaze me when you don't break the peel." I watched her accomplish the task on two more.

She cut the apples into slices, discarded the cores and seeds and chopped the slices into chunks. "Years of practice. I learned the trick from my grandmother, or she passed on the genetic skill. At any rate, I want to make more apple butter for Saturday. Plus, some jars of applesauce. I had several people inquire about it last week. At least they've taken down the police tape, so it won't draw attention when we open on Saturday. Have you been back to the river?"

"No. I should head there this afternoon and make sure the area is free of debris or whatever people left behind."

A white truck with *Winter's* scrolled on the side rolled into the barnyard. Johnson trundled out of the driver's side and waved. "I'd better meet him." I stepped off the porch and joined him beside the barn. "Morning, Mr. Winters." I extended my hand to shake, but he craned his neck to see the damage at the top of the door.

"I need my ladder." He loped to the truck, pulled his aluminum ladder from the rack, carried it to the barn, and leaned it against the red wood siding. He tugged on the tram. "Mighty loose. You need more support." He climbed from the top and jumped to the ground from the third step. "Let me check inside."

Spry for an older fellow. I followed him into the barn.

He pointed above the door. "You've had rain come in around the bolt, and it rotted the part of the wall the tram is attached to. I can add wood and stabilize the area, then reattach the tram. That should take care of the leak too. I'll need a piece of lumber, but the metal itself appears in good shape." We walked back to the truck, where he hooked the ladder. He wrote on a pad he nabbed from the cab. "Here's an estimate. If you agree, I'll be back tomorrow morning and make it as good as new. Well, as close as I can."

On the paper, he'd written a quote lower than I expected. "Is this for labor, too?"

"Sure is. I'm hoping you'll recommend me to your friends." He tipped his Seattle Mariners baseball cap.

An unsettled twitch in my gut left me uncertain of how to inquire into his relationship with Marcy or the mayor, and Aunt Cordy wanted the door repaired, so I confirmed his services. "My aunt appreciated the repair you completed on her barn roof. Who else have you worked for in town?"

He studied his boots, then looked me in the eye. "The folks in the big yellow house on Bluebird Trail asked me to install new windows on the bottom floor. With a house as yellow as theirs, they should live on Canary Street." He howled with laughter. I chuckled out of politeness.

I tilted my head. "Did you do any work for Mayor Richardson?"

He shifted his gaze to the left. "No. I hadn't met him. It's a shame he passed." His neck reddened. He'd lied to me.

"I saw you talking to Marcy Fox at the festival. Would she give you a good reference?" I watched him as he paused to answer.

He nodded. "Yes. I installed shelves for her at her shop. She was pleased with my work."

"Great, then I'll see you tomorrow."

"I'll be here at nine in the morning."

"Sounds good. Thank you."

He tapped on the hood of his truck. "I'd best get to my next job. Thanks for trusting me with your door." He climbed into his truck and kicked up dust in the driveway on his way out.

On the porch, I shared the estimate with my aunt. "He's undercharging. Labor alone costs more with most contractors. He says he's trying to build business and find reputable recommendations. Understandable, but I asked if he'd done any work for Mayor Richardson. He said no, and he'd not met him. I'm going to go through the photos again. I'm sure he stood beside him in one of them."

"I'll be in the kitchen cooking these apples down. Let me know what you find." In the house, I hurried up the stairs, and she headed to the kitchen. Half an hour later, the house smelled of apples and cinnamon. My nose led me to the kitchen where Aunt Cordy joined me at the table to study the photos I'd printed.

I handed her a color print. "In this one, Johnson Winters is standing beside the mayor. They're listening to Zach explain the apple bobbing booth and see this one."

"They're discussing something, and it doesn't seem friendly." Behind Aunt Cordy's tent, the mayor's finger pointed at Winters' face. Mr. Winters' eyes bulged, and his cheeks reddened.

She handed the photo back to me. "Why would he lie to me?"

Steam swirled above the kettle of apples. Aunt Cordy squinted her eyes as if in deep thought. She stirred the apples, and I breathed in the fragrance of her sweet applesauce. "What motive does Johnson Winters have? Even if he lied to you, why would he want the mayor dead?"

I dipped a spoon into the mushy apples and spread some on a saltine cracker. The sweetness and saltiness satisfied my palate. "He's trying to build a business. Could be the mayor interfered with a job, or a licensing, or even an inspection. Mayor Richardson took his job seriously, probably too much so." I pointed the spoon at Aunt Cordy. “What if Luna Pascal was seeking revenge on the mayor for her Aunt June?”

She stirred the sauce. “Did you talk to Otis? He and the mayor were at war all the time.”

“I may ask Laurel to speak to him. She can go in with the premise of writing for her blog.” I washed my spoon and put it into the drainer. “If you don’t need me for a while, I’m going to take the sheep to the field near the river and poke around. They can graze while I take some photos and check out the area.”

I fetched my camera and went to gather Floss and Thimble. “Come on, girls. Let’s take a walk.” The two beauties followed me along a path to the field beside the river. Content to munch on the grass, I left them to graze.

At the edge of the old foundation where Zach and I had discovered the mayor’s body, I paused. A shiver crawled along my spine. Was someone watching me? I shook off the creepy feeling, when I peered over my shoulder and saw the sheep. A pungent burnt-wood odor drifted past my nose but then whisked away on the breeze.

The police had removed the tape, but their feet had crunched the grass, and remnants of yellow plastic littered the area. Gold and scarlet leaves had tumbled from the trees during yesterday’s rain. Before I moved past the perimeter, I snapped photos. The lens focused on the angles from outside the foundation and the structure left of the old home place’s walls. I stood in the opening where I had fallen and perused the inside. The police had confiscated the apple butter paddle. I treaded around the inside perimeter, snapping pictures as I went. The sun glinted on something. My toe kicked at a tuft of grass and revealed a silver tube. With my hand wrapped in my sleeve, I lifted it from the ground. Ridges ran around the sides, with a closed end. I shoved it in my pocket to examine later.

Floss and Thimble baaed and jingled the bells on their necks. I trekked back to the field to check on them. Zach stood beside them and petted their fluff.

He jogged to meet me. "Cordy told me you were out here. Find anything interesting?"

I pulled the tube from my pocket with the cuff of my sleeve. "This was under a pile of leaves. Could be a lipstick tube, but I haven't opened it."

Zach stared at it. "You may want to give it to your brother-in-law."

"Yeah. I should." I tucked it into my pocket, and we headed back to the river.

He tapped my shoulder. "Do you smell smoke?"

Once he brought it to my attention, I did. Not a strong scent, but smoky. "I caught a whiff of smoke earlier, but it dissipated so fast I didn't pay it any mind." He followed his nose, and I followed him. Along the bank near the old foundation, a campfire had been burning. Someone had doused it, and a few smoke tendrils drifted with the breeze.

"Someone may have been here, and I didn't see them. When I walked back to the field, they must have run." I crossed my arms over the camera strap hanging around my neck. "Sometimes people camp here and take apples. Aunt Cordy says as long as they cause no harm, she doesn't mind, but a fire could cause problems."

Zach used his boot to cover the ashes with dirt. "Last thing we need is a fire. Do you suppose someone was watching the area since Saturday?"

I shrugged. "Anything is possible." Once Zach assured me the ashes had cooled, I invited him to poke around the area, in case he saw something I missed. We shoved damp leaves aside but found nothing interesting until we sat on the edge of the wall. Zach laid his hand on the stone, and a piece of denim fabric fell to the ground. "What's this?" He used his sleeve to pick the fabric up without touching it.

He flipped the piece over. "Looks too thin for jeans material."

I photographed it and zoomed in. "Yeah. Might be a shirt or jacket. It's a lighter shade of blue too. Do you remember anyone wearing a denim shirt at the festival on Saturday?"

He slipped the fabric into his shirt pocket. "Never paid much attention to what people wore."

I lifted my camera and called up the digital photos from Saturday. "I haven't deleted any of my pictures. Let's flip through and see if we find someone in this color."

One by one, we rolled through the photos. Two people wore light-blue denim shirts. Jonquil Rose and Aunt Cordy. "Oh boy. I'd hoped we'd find Marcy in blue, not my aunt."

"Let's walk back to the house. I'm sure there's an explanation." Zach and I gathered the sheep and led them back to the barn. They trotted into their pen and slurped water.

In the house, we found Aunt Cordy pouring applesauce into jars. The fragrance of cinnamon and nutmeg hung in the air. I watched my aunt spoon the pale-yellow sauce in each jar and tighten the lids. Using a jar lifter, she dropped each jar into a bath of boiling water to seal them. She hummed and smiled as she worked. Oh, how I hated to break into her peaceful world.

Chapter Ten

Once Aunt Cordy lowered the last jar of applesauce into the hot water bath, she placed a lid on the pan and carried the utensils to the sink. Hot water poured from the faucet, and suds bubbled from the dish soap. Her humming had turned to song as she belted out Sweet Caroline, with emphasis on the bom, bom, boms. When she lifted a wooden spoon to her lips to use as a microphone, I cleared my throat. She grabbed the front of her neck and turned to me. "What are you doing?"

"I'm so sorry. We didn't mean to startle you." I squeezed her hand. "The applesauce smells amazing."

She untucked a chair from the table and sat. "Thank you. I made six jars of sauce and six apple butter. My feet hurt. I'm not used to standing in one place for long. I can walk all day, but standing still gets me every time." She massaged the calf on her right leg.

I didn't want to ask her about the denim scrap we had found. My eyes met Zach's. He shrugged and then reached into his pocket and extracted the ragged patch. My aunt eyed us, and her brow wrinkled. "What have you got?"

Zach and I joined her at the table. I fingered the doily under a bowl of fruit. “When we walked to the river, we poked around and didn’t find much until we sat on the rock wall.” I nudged the cloth toward my aunt. “This fell from a crack in the wall. We think it’s from a denim shirt.”

Aunt Cordy lifted the cloth from the table. “I believe this is mine. A few weeks ago, I wandered to the old remnants of the cabin and sat on the rocks. Sometimes, I sit there and watch the river and pray. When I stood, my shirttail caught in a groove and tore. I didn’t bother to search for the ripped-out piece. I lost my favorite lipstick too.” Her eyes widened. “Did you think it made me guilty?”

Zach and I exchanged glances. “In the photos, only you and Jonquil had on denim shirts the color of this.” I held the fabric in front of her.

“Just so you know, I bought a new shirt to replace the ripped one, and I wear the other one when I work in the orchard.” She stood and walked to the stove where she turned the burner off and moved the hot bath to a different one. She laid out a towel on the counter, then lifted the jars one by one from the pot. The jars popped as they cooled, a sign they had sealed.

I joined her at the stove. “I’m sorry, but we had to ask. I’m thankful it was from weeks ago, and we found it instead of Danny.” I carried the pot of hot water to the sink and dumped it. Steam rose in my face and clouded the glasses I’d worn instead of my contacts.

Aunt Cordy waved her hand. "No worries. I understand, and this takes Jonquil off the hook, too." We hugged, and I kissed her on the forehead. She was the sweetest person, and I cherished her understanding and patience. When I first came home, she sat up with me at night when I had nightmares. After a month and a few chats with a counselor, the nightmares slowed. In every one of them, Elias held my hand and then disappeared into a hole. My screams had awakened my aunt, and she held me until I had fallen asleep. I'd never accuse her of anything horrendous, especially murder, so I'm glad she gave us reason to toss the denim scrap.

I dried the pan and put it in the pantry. A bump against the cabinet reminded me of the tube in my pocket. I extracted it and handed it to my aunt. "Is this yours?"

She spun it between her fingers, then uncapped the tube. "Sure is. It's seen better days. I'll buy a new one." She tossed it into the trash.

"By the way, we took Floss and Thimble with us, and they stayed close by and grazed in the field. From what I've read, the Valais Blacknose sheep respond to their owners like a pet, which means they'll follow me around and play." I hadn't owned a pet since our dog, Cobbler. The little mutt lived with us in Guatemala and trailed after Laurel and me everywhere.

Zach remained at the table and stared at his cell phone. "Um. You might want to see this." He held his phone out so we could read it.

An article in the local newspaper blasted the Apple Festival for being unsafe. They claimed the mayor died because he tripped and fell on a rock and hit his head, after he had eaten pie from Aunt Cordy's booth. "What? Who wrote that?"

"Oh no." Aunt Cordy gripped the back of the chair.

Zach scrolled to the top of the article. "Raleigh Leicester is the writer. Any idea who he is?"

"No, but I'm going to find him. You want to come with me?" My eyes pierced Zach. Anger bubbled inside me. How could someone write untruths and publish them? They hurt people, and today they hurt my aunt. I turned to Aunt Cordy. "We'll be back."

Zach followed me outdoors, where we climbed into my Jeep. I started the engine and drove away from the homestead. "Zach, I'm sorry to draw you into this mess, but I need a second set of ears to make sure I don't say anything I shouldn't. Please stop me if you hear me going off. I want to get this corrected and understand why the newspaper was so sloppy."

He pressed a hand to my shoulder. "It's fine. I want to help, especially your aunt. She's been so kind to me, and so have you. I'm glad I'm available today. Tomorrow is a twelve-hour day. We have several classes coming to the education center, then I have a presentation at the garden club to talk about native plants."

"Has anyone told you your voice has a calming quality?" I sent a smile his way.

He dropped his chin to his chest, then raised it with a shy glimpse at me. "No, but I appreciate it, and I'm thankful I can help in a small way."

I pulled into a parking spot in front of the newspaper office. "Here goes." We climbed out of the Jeep and entered the building. At the front desk, a man with shoulder-length curls and a full beard typed on his computer. With narrowed eyes, he peered over the monitor, his fingers flying across the keyboard. "Can I help you?" The clicking stopped, and he rose from his chair.

No one else worked in the small office today. "We're looking for Raleigh Leicester."

"You found him." He pushed his hair behind his ears. "Want to stand or sit at the conference table?" He gestured to a small round table in the corner with three straight-back chairs, maybe something from IKEA.

I marched past the reporter, and the men followed. "We read an article online about the mayor's death." Zach called it up on his phone and showed it to Raleigh. He glanced over it.

"Yeah. I wrote it." He leaned away from us and crossed his leg over his knee.

"It's inaccurate, and I want you to write a retraction, then tell the truth." My voice rose at the end of the sentence. Zach laid his hand on my arm. I nodded to him, and he let go. "The mayor didn't trip and hit his head or have issues with my aunt's pie. Someone hit him with an apple butter paddle and knocked him to the ground. He may have hit his head then, but your article makes it sound like Aunt Cordy's pie made him fall down. Your words shone a poor light on our apple festival." I took a deep breath.

Raleigh rubbed his beard. "Otis Reardon spilled this story to me."

"Don't you fact check? Did you interview the police? Or even bother to talk to my aunt?" I crossed my arms.

He leaned forward with his elbows on the table. "I tried to talk to the police, and they didn't have time to chat. Otis is an upstanding citizen, so I figured he'd told me the truth."

I stood with my hands on my hips. "I was a war correspondent for twenty years, and if I'd turned in an article without the facts, I'd have been in hot water, as they say. Trust me, when a country is at war, it's not always easy to get to the truth. I'd think in a town the size of Seldom Seen, you'd be able to find a reliable source. Besides, Otis...never mind." Zach stood beside me. "We want a retraction in the next print and online edition of the paper and a free ad for the apple festival—run tomorrow. Saturday and Sunday we want folks to come to the homestead to pick apples and have fun."

Raleigh nodded and stood. "Can do. I'm sorry. I was in a hurry and failed to check out the facts. You may want to talk to Otis, who is spreading the story around town faster than my article. Please tell your aunt I'm sorry." He reached his hand out to shake. "If you don't mind, I have a question." He didn't hesitate. "Why aren't you in the field now?"

I shook and released his hand, as did Zach. "It was time for a change." I turned and beelined to my Jeep.

Zach climbed in. I rested my head on the steering wheel. His hand touched my elbow. "Hey. You did great. I'm surprised he agreed to retract the story without much fight."

I raised my head from the steering wheel and stared at Zach. "I intimidated him with my years of experience. He may have feared I'd turn him into the publisher or report him for slander. He appeared pretty young, early twenties. Will you watch for a retraction?"

"Of course." He buckled his seatbelt while I pulled into the street. "I never dreamed I'd be involved in a murder investigation when I left Ohio, but I know what it's like to be accused of something you didn't do."

"Thank you. I'm sorry you went through a tough time." We drove a few blocks and parked. I gripped the steering wheel. "We could have walked, but I needed a few minutes to pull myself together. Driving helps me settle." I opened the visor mirror and saw where red rimmed my eyes from lack of sleep. I blinked a few times. Oh, well. "Let's go see Otis."

Inside Toolsmith Hardware, Otis bent over the counter. As we approached, I noticed a newspaper spread out in front of him. "Good afternoon." We approached the man. Zach stepped in front of me.

"What are you reading?" Zach placed a hand on either side of the newspaper. "Wouldn't be the article you fed to Raleigh

Leicester, would it?" He tapped on the paper. "No, Raleigh posted the one you shared on the website for the world to see."

Otis stared at Zach. He jutted his chin out. "All I did was share what I heard."

I gave Zach the floor. He pounded the counter once with his fist. "What you were told wasn't true, and it could hurt Cordelia Benton's festival. Why would you drag her name through the mud? The article implied the mayor ate her pie, and it made him fall and hit his head. That's a lie." My friend backed away from the counter and motioned for me to take over. The man should be riding a white steed.

I stepped to the counter and used my most intense glare. "Explain yourself."

Otis raised his face to the ceiling, then he lowered his eyes to rest on me. "June told me what happened. She said she was at the festival and saw the whole thing. After she left, Raleigh stopped in to pick up a hammer and nails. I asked him if he'd heard the entire story, then I spilled June's version. I left the festival before the mayor had died, so I wasn't around."

"Neither was June. No one but our family stayed late." I pointed my finger at him. "You should know better than to believe June after she ruined the mural. Good grief, she might be responsible and trying to throw everyone off her trail." I huffed and Zach placed a hand on my back. "We spoke to Raleigh, and he's to print a retraction, but you, sir, should apologize to my aunt. This put her in a negative light. And you better be telling everyone you see you were wrong." I crossed my arms. "By the way, don't bother to come to the festival, because your booth will be given to someone else." I turned and strode out of the hardware store. Seven customers stood with their mouths open. Yes, I counted them and proceeded to count to ten to get myself under control.

Chapter Eleven

The sun slipped beyond the horizon as I drove Zach to the homestead, while the wind whipped our hair through the open windows. Frogs croaked as the sun's last rays gave light to the orange and purple sky, and chimney smoke drifted into the Jeep.

We ribboned along the driveway and parked in the barnyard. I rolled my window up as Zach did the same. No automatic windows or locks in my vintage vehicle. We unbuckled the seat belts and got out. I sniffed the air as we neared the porch. "We forgot to ask Aunt Cordy about the campfire we found."

Zach nodded, and my aunt's voice called to us. "What campfire?" She rested in a porch rocker with a blanket over her.

We settled into the chairs beside her. "We'll tell you in a minute." I filled her in on our conversations with Raleigh and Otis and assured her Raleigh would promote her festival.

"What a relief. Did Otis say why he told the newspaper reporter what he did?" She folded her hands over the blanket in her lap.

My rocker click-clacked against the wood. "June told him."

"That woman. Why on earth?"

A rumble echoed from Zach's direction.

"Someone is hungry. You two haven't had time to eat today. I fixed a plate of sandwiches." Aunt Cordy stood and folded her blanket. "Be right back."

In two minutes, she returned with a tray of bologna salad sandwiches and iced tea. Laurel and I had eaten a ton of these sandwiches as kids. The tangy Miracle Whip, sweet pickles, hard-boiled eggs, and bologna combined to make a tasty treat. My mom had shared how her grandmother taught her to make it. My friend's mom used ham, but I preferred bologna. I bit into it. Did I savor the bite because I was so hungry or because of childhood memories? "Delicious."

Zach examined his sandwich. "Um. What is this?"

"The best sandwich you'll ever eat." I took another bite. Oh, how I had missed my family's recipes when I lived abroad. Of course, I had eaten many interesting dishes and enjoyed much of it, but nothing matched my aunt's home cooking.

Zach chewed a bite of the sandwich. "Mmm. Tasty."

"You've never eaten bologna salad?" I sipped my tea.

He shook his head and ate more. After he swallowed, he lifted a corner of the bread. "Different from anything I've tasted before, but I like it."

We chuckled, then I pointed at Zach. "I forgot to tell you how Zach spoke to Otis with authority. We have ourselves a man who stands for truth and justice."

He smiled at my aunt. "It was nothing. I don't want to see anyone blamed for something they didn't do. Especially you."

He finished the last bite of his sandwich. "Back to the campfire. When we walked to the river, we found a partially burned campfire. Someone had snuffed it out, but heat rose from the ashes. I doused it with dirt."

My aunt tapped her finger on her chin. "Could be anyone. People camp there without permission from time to time, but I wonder if it's someone connected to the mayor. They may watch us to see what the police find or what we do." She raised her eyebrows and pointed her finger at me. "Lyndie Louise Lavender, I don't want you walking to the river alone for now. Anyone might be around."

"I understand, but I spent twenty years in much more dangerous places." I got up and gathered the remnants of supper. "I'm ready to head to bed. It's early, but I'm tired."

Zach walked to the porch steps. "Goodnight, ladies. I'll be busy tomorrow, but you can call if you need me."

"Thanks, Zach." Aunt Cordy waved to him and then followed me into the house. "He's such a kind young man."

"He is." At my aunt's white porcelain sink, I washed the plates and utensils. After I dried the last fork, I kissed Aunt Cordy on the cheek. "Night. I'll see you in the morning."

"Goodnight." She slipped off to her bedroom.

Upstairs, I drew out my notebook and jotted down everything we discovered today. The knot of confusion tightened as far as who killed the mayor. Tomorrow I'd make an effort to chat with my sister and Danny.

#####

Friday morning, the bleats of Floss and Thimble, and Happy and Bashful sounded through the kitchen's open window. A cool breeze tossed the curtains as I poured myself a cup of coffee. A peace I'd not encountered in a long time coursed through me, even as I contemplated how to approach my brother-in-law about the mayor's death. According to Laurel, the police determined the death a homicide, so a killer roamed the countryside. My gut told me the person was someone we knew, yet I couldn't imagine anyone on our list harming another person on purpose, no matter how angry they were.

I carried my coffee to the table where I had laid my notebook with the list of suspects. Otis, June, Marcy, Johnson Winters, Aunt Cordy. I scribbled her name off of the list. Certain we'd missed someone, I left the house and searched for my aunt. She stood on the porch with her watering can, dousing the flowers.

"Morning." She smiled and rested the watering can on the step.

"Good morning. After I finish my morning chores, I plan to drive into town to talk to Danny and see if he'll share any information on the mayor's case. I'm guessing he won't, but it's worth asking. Then I'm going to see Laurel."

My aunt frowned and held a hand on her hip. "You forgot about Johnson Winters, didn't you?"

I smacked my hand against my forehead. "I sure did. He's coming to fix the barn door, isn't he? I'll need to move the sheep and goats away from the barn. I'm sorry."

"I'd do it, but Walt is coming over for lunch." A smile and a hint of a dreamy look crossed her face.

I bit my lip to stop a giggle. "No worries. I'll hang here until he finishes with the barn door. I'll take the animals to the grassy pasture. I've been wanting to photograph them anyway. Then, I'll head to town. Thanks for the reminder, and you and Walt have a delightful lunch."

She shooed me to the barn after I grabbed my camera.

#####

My new friends, in their fluffy robes, nuzzled my legs. I petted their heads and led them out of their shelter to join the goats. We roamed to the meadow on the other side of their fenced area. Floss and Thimble tumbled along behind me while Happy and Bashful jumped and butted heads. Aunt Cordy had told me they bump each other with their heads to get attention, show dominance, or play. From what I'd witnessed, Bashful appeared the dominant one. I let them play while I searched for the best spot to take photos.

The Winters' truck rumbled along the driveway, then stopped beside the barn. I made sure the animals were secure in the field, then met the handyman.

He raised his hand and waved, then climbed out of his truck. "Morning. You've got some pretty sheep there." He pulled a ladder from the rack of the truck and lugged it and a toolbox to the barn.

"Thank you. They're fun to have around." I walked with him to the broken door.

He leaned the ladder on the wall of the barn. "This shouldn't take too long." He eyed the camera around my neck. "You going to photograph me while I work? I should have worn a nicer shirt." He tugged at the hem of his stained t-shirt.

I glanced at my camera. "No." A laugh escaped me. "I'm going to take pictures of the animals and keep them away from the barn while you work."

"I appreciate it. Last thing I need is to get headbutted by a goat. One got me when I was a kid, and it hurt." He searched through the toolbox. "Have you heard anything else about the mayor's murder?"

The question rolled off his tongue as if he'd lived in Seldom Seen his entire life. Where had he lived? "I haven't." No need to share anything with a person on the suspect list.

I had never been creative with small talk, instead I tended to blurt things out. "Where did you grow up, Mr. Winters?"

He dropped his hammer on his foot. A yell and then a few words I wouldn't repeat escaped his mouth, and the sheep bleated. "Sorry. Man, that hurt." He leaned over and rubbed the top of his boot.

I'm not sure how rubbing his boot helped. "Do you want something for pain or some ice?"

"No, I'll be okay. The boots have steel toes, but it hit higher on my foot." He walked across the barn lot and back. "I'm good."

"Okay. If you need anything, I'll be in the field with the animals." I nodded my head and jogged to the sheep. So much for discovering where he had lived. I would ask Marcy, but she wouldn't speak to me.

Floss and Thimble twisted and turned, trotted the other way, and stuck out their tongues a few times. Once they found some weeds to munch on, I captured several worthy shots. Happy and Bashful photobombed them, so I moved my attention to them and caught them play fighting and bouncing about. All to the rhythm of a hammer.

An hour later, Johnson Winters rounded the corner of the barn and hiked to the meadow where the animals played.

I ambled to him. "All finished?"

He paused at the gate. "Yes. It wasn't a big job." He held a piece of paper in his hand. "Here's the bill. Do you want it, or should I leave it at the house?"

"I'll take it." He passed the yellow slip to me. "Are you sure this is enough?" He'd lowballed the price.

"Positive. I had some of the wood I needed, and I reused the metalwork from the barn. Plus, it didn't take long."

"Let me take a look before you go." I wanted to make sure his work met my aunt's standards, and mine too.

He led me to the front of the barn. Sure enough, the door hung straight and slid back and forth with ease. "Excellent. Thank you so much."

A grin crossed his face. "I do my best. Been at this for forty years, so I best get it right." Interesting. He had told Zach he had an environmental background. Was he lying?

He had already packed his tools and ladder on his truck, so I reached out and shook his hand. “I’ll be sure and give Aunt Cordy the bill and you a glowing review on Laurel’s site.”

“I appreciate it. You have a good day.” He turned to the truck, and I returned to the animals.

In the field, I gathered the sheep and goats and led them back to the pasture behind the barn. Tired from their intense photo session, they all plopped to the ground and fell asleep. Oh, to be an animal and sleep whenever you wanted.

Walt had parked his truck near the house. Inside, without disturbing the couple, I tucked the bill under the corner of Aunt Cordy’s bowl for keys then climbed the steps to my room and changed into clean jeans. In my foray with the sheep, I’d knelt in mud. At least I hoped it was mud. After I changed, I rested on the edge of the bed and flipped through the photos of Thimble, Floss, Happy, and Bashful. In one of them, Johnson Winters stood at the corner of the barn and watched us. Creepy. Maybe he waited for me to finish, but even then, it gave me chills. He’d accomplished his task on the barn door and remained polite, but I didn’t trust him. Something about his grin left me uncomfortable. Did he drop the hammer on his foot to keep from answering my question about where he had lived? What if he had a secret past? Good grief. I sounded like my sister. *Chill, Lyndie.*

Before I let my imagination grow, I placed my camera in the case and then hustled down the steps and out the door to my Jeep.

It was time to talk to Danny.

Chapter Twelve

For a Friday afternoon, I found the streets empty, and the sidewalks deserted. I parked in front of the police department. Someone had painted the old brick a soft blue-gray, a pleasant shade for a place where the occupants dealt with lawbreakers and crime. As I got out of my car, I watched Danny hurry into the building where I intended to speak to him.

Inside, the cream walls contrasted with a mahogany counter and several dark-gray desks. Officer Helena Ashton typed on a computer at the front desk, but I didn't see Marge, the fifty-something administrative assistant.

Helena raised her head when I approached the desk. "Hi. Would it be okay for me to speak to Danny?" I nodded toward his office. The plate on his door announced his sergeant rank and investigative officer status. He had spent years earning his rank. Laurel glowed with pride anytime someone acknowledged his achievement.

The blond woman with a pixie cut stood her whole five foot three and knocked on the door to my brother-in-law's office. My brother-in-law's voice rumbled from the other room. Helena turned to me. "He said to go in."

"Thanks." I peered around the door to find Danny alone, bent over his desk, writing on a yellow legal pad. Good.

He raised his head and peered at me. The dark shadows under his eyes told the story of his weariness. I couldn't imagine the stress he lived with. "Hi, Lyndie. Come in." I stepped into the room and snapped the door closed. He waved to a chair, and I took a seat. "How are you and Aunt Cordy doing?"

"We're good. We'd be better though if we found who murdered the mayor." My bluntness ruled again.

He nodded and flipped his pen in his fingers. "I hear you. We'd all be more comfortable at this point. I can tell you the police are doing everything to follow the evidence with the intent of making an arrest."

While Danny spoke, I pulled my notebook from my bag. "I appreciate all you're doing. I...um...wondered if I could share some observations I've noticed." Did that make sense?

He narrowed his gaze. "I told you, I don't want you or Laurel getting mixed up in this. I remember how nosy you two were in high school. When Mr. Willman's grandson, Jordan, came for a visit, you two sneaked onto their property and eavesdropped under the window to see if you could find out if Jordan had a girlfriend."

"Not my proudest moment, but we had promised our best friend, Julia, we'd find out." Heat rose up from my neck to my face. "High school was a long time ago. You can trust me, and I might bring a fresh perspective." Perspiration trickled down my back as I waited to share what I had heard.

He sighed a big breath. "Fine. What do you have?"

"June and Otis are spreading rumors." I flipped a page in my notebook to make sure I repeated the correct information. "June claimed the mayor ate Aunt Cordy's pie, and it made him sick and caused him to fall and hit his head on a rock. Raleigh Leicester, a reporter at our local paper, posted the story online. I visited him this morning and told him to retract it." I caught my breath. "June is also saying the Apple Festival is dangerous and will make people sick. I don't understand what's happened with her. Her kindness has turned to poison."

Danny penned notes in his pad. "June changed after she was arrested for destroying the mural. Although she didn't do jail time, I think her shame messed with her. What else have you got?"

Danny's observations of June made sense. She had worked for the mayor, so perhaps she felt she needed to defend his honor. "Johnson Winters came by to work on the barn, and after he finished, he watched me photograph my sheep. I have a picture of him peeking around the corner of the barn at us." I stood and paced the small space.

Danny placed his pen on the desk. "Did you ask him why he was watching?"

"No. I didn't realize he was until I scanned through the photos later in my room." I sat on the chair. "Did you look through the pictures I sent you?"

"I did."

"Did you notice the tall man in the fedora and long coat?" I folded my hands in my lap.

"Hold on." He called up the shots I'd taken. "Step around here."

I leaned over his shoulder and watched as he moved from one to the next. "There. Him. Who is he? Have you seen him in town?"

Danny tapped his finger on the screen. "Yeah. I've seen him. I recognize the hat. The red feather gives him away. Laurel said his name is Greg Garrison."

"Who is he?"

"I haven't met him, but I think he's staying at Mrs. Rawlin's rental. She's got a small house on Juniper Street. He walks around town, but I've no idea if or where he works." He sighed. "Just because he's in the pictures doesn't make him a suspect, but I'll try to find out more about him. In the meantime, stay out of the investigation. Lieutenant Jackson and I will find out what happened."

I tucked my notebook into my bag. "One more thing. Someone lit a campfire on Aunt Cordy's property yesterday. Zach and I found it, and it was still warm. You might want to check it out." I didn't mention the blue fabric scrap or lipstick tube since they belonged to my aunt.

"I'll see what I can do." He turned his head to the computer.

I'd been dismissed.

#####

A few more people traversed Seldom Seen's sidewalks, when I left, and one of them happened to be the man in the fedora with the red feather. He ducked into Baker's Delight. Time to spy… I mean gather information. I had skipped lunch and could use a sugary, chocolate pick me up. Through the window, I saw Mr. Fedora peer into the display case. Delight Brooks, the owner, scooped three cookies from a tray and secured them in a white wax bag. He stepped to the register, and I slid into the store. The smell of freshly baked goods tickled my appetite. Once I recovered from a longing to chase the smells, I made a show of ogling the walnut brownies. My mouth watered.

The mystery man handed Delight a fifty-dollar bill. Big money for a small town. "Thanks so much." He patted her hand after she made change.

"You're welcome, Mr. Garrison." The man turned, tipped his hat to me, and left.

"Hi, Lyndie. How can I help you?" Delight wore her long brown hair in a braided bun and pushed a few loose wisps behind her ear. Dressed in a pink and white striped t-shirt and a teal apron, she represented her store brand well.

With my curiosity at its peak, I held my questions for a minute. "I'd like a walnut brownie. Yours are the absolute best."

"I appreciate your compliment, but I bet you've eaten amazing pastries all over the world." She bagged the brownie. "Anything else?"

"A carton of skim milk would be perfect." I loved milk but found my stomach only tolerated the nonfat kind. At home, I kept a carton of almond milk for my coffee.

No one else entered the bakery, so after I paid, I leaned over the counter and used my indoor voice. "Do you know Mr. Garrison?"

Delight scrunched her forehead, squinted her eyes, and tilted her head. "Not well. Why do you ask?"

I chewed my lower lip. How did I tell her I started investigating the mayor's murder without my brother-in-law's permission? "I took some photos at the Apple Fest, and he showed up in a few of them. I didn't recognize him at first, so I wondered who he was."

She moved a few items to the front of the display cabinets, then slid the door closed. "Makes sense. His name is Greg Garrison. He told me he had come to Seldom Seen to rest and relax, something about a sabbatical. From what I've seen, he hangs around town all day. He stops here every day and buys a treat and a coffee." She adjusted a loose bobby pin in her hair. "He's pleasant and leaves a generous tip. He could be about our age, don't you think? And he wears his fedora every day, no matter the weather." She tapped her finger on her lip. "I wonder if he's bald on top." A giggle bubbled from her throat.

"Has he been here long?" My inquisitiveness may give me away.

"He came into the shop in early September. I've seen him on the walking path on the weekends. He nods and smiles. Not much of a talker."

"I don't suppose he's told you how long he's staying." The frown on her face told me I'd asked one too many questions.

"Are you interested in meeting him? I thought you'd have your eye on your cute tenant. What's his name? Zach?" She winked.

Good grief. I didn't have time for any of what she suggested. "No. I'm simply curious."

"He mentioned Mrs. Rawlin's mashed potatoes and gravy the other day. Must be staying there." Her lips twisted into a broad grin.

The bell jingled on the door as a mom and her little one entered. "I'll see you later. Have a good rest of your day." I flitted out of the shop and ambled to my car.

I drove the Jeep to the other end of town and parked in front of the office Danny's dad owned and Laurel worked out of. The half hour before she picked up her kids from school gave me enough time to chat with her.

At the push of the door, Laurel rose from her desk. "Hey, sister. What are you doing? Shouldn't you be preparing for tomorrow?"

"I left Aunt Cordy with Walt. They had lunch. Most everything is still set from last weekend, other than adding tablecloths and a few other small items to the tables. I'm guessing Walt is helping her."

Laurel took my hand and guided me to the table in the back corner. No one else worked at the other two computer stations. Laurel created content for the Seldom Seen web page, and two other people rented space to work on their own internet businesses. "Sit with me. I'm finished for the day and waiting to pick up the kids from school."

"I hoped I'd catch you before you left." We sat at the round table in the back corner. "I found out June and Otis had spread rumors about Aunt Cordy."

"I read that awful article online this morning."

"Raleigh Leichester is putting in a retraction." I took the white paper bag with my brownie from my purse. "Want half?" I offered part of it to my sister even though my stomach told my head to eat the whole thing.

"Sure. Let me grab some water." She handed me a chilled bottle from her small fridge.

"Thanks." I bit into the chocolaty goodness. "Yum. Nothing like Delight's baked goods. Anyway, I talked to Raleigh and he's going to print a retraction. After I saw him, I stopped in to talk to Danny. He told me to stay out of the investigation." I chewed another bite. "Did he tell you anything?"

"Nope. Nothing. I didn't even hear him talking on the phone." She sipped her water.

"I asked him about the guy in the fedora I showed you in the photos, then I ran into the man. Kind of. He had entered Baker's Delight, and I followed him. He paid with a fifty. I asked Delight about him, and her response concurred with what Danny told me. He's staying at Mrs. Rawlin's. He's not working, and he said he was here to relax. Delight wondered if I was interested in him." I took the last bite of brownie.

"Are you?"

"Am I what?"

"Interested in him." She licked her fingers.

"No. Why would I be? I don't know the man." I shook my head and handed her a napkin from the pile on the table. "Zach and I found a campfire on Aunt Cordy's property. I told Danny about it. He's going to check it out."

"Do we need to figure out a way to question the mystery man in the fedora?"

I capped my water bottle after I finished drinking. "One of us can chat with him if he comes to the festival again." I used air quotes for the word chat. "We may discover more information about him. Like, was he familiar with the mayor?"

"Sounds reasonable." She glanced at the clock on the wall. "I'd better pick up the kiddos." We hugged. "Talk later."

"Will do. I'm excited for Josephine and Henry to show off Floss and Thimble tomorrow. Those sheep will enjoy the attention."

"So will my children. They have fallen in love with those beautiful creatures." She wrapped a lace shawl around her shoulders.

"I have too. They are such good listeners and soothers of my soul." I held the door open for her, then bid her goodbye.

On the drive to the homestead, I ruminated over the information I had gathered today. As little as it was, it might make a difference in the case.

Chapter Thirteen

On Saturday morning at seven, the sun peeked over the mountains as Zack, Laurel, and I ate muffins and drank butter pecan coffee on the front porch. Rays of gold and orange awakened the sky and me. The Apple Fest started in a couple of hours, and although Walt had helped Aunt Cordy yesterday, as I had hoped, we still wanted to add the final touches.

After we finished breakfast, Zach and I delivered tablecloths to Aunt Cordy and Laurel to cover the tables beside the food trucks and the tables scattered throughout the center of the festival. In Danny's absence, Zach carried the pan of water to the apple bobbing booth. Laurel had hinted Danny planned to attend in uniform and scope out the people.

By eight-thirty, most of the vendors had completed setup. I checked on Josephine and Henry. In reality, I longed to pet Floss and Thimble. A sense of calm flowed through me when I ran my hands over their luxurious fluff. My buddies stood inside a low fence with Bashful and Happy. One of our neighbors tethered his small pony to a post, while Josephine and Henry herded the chickens into a pen. I leaned over the fence and petted my girls. They baaed and rubbed their heads against my hand. How did I get by without these beauties before? The Lord knew I needed extra comfort in my life. Again, I thanked him for my aunt and her little farm.

At nine o'clock, car tires kicked the dust on the long driveway. The murder hadn't kept folks from coming to the festival. Perhaps curiosity drove a few to attend. At any rate, I hoped they would support our local vendors and my aunt.

I checked the apple-bobbing booth. Zach had recruited his cousin Jeremiah to work in the booth today. He owned an outfitters business in town, Appalachian Adventures, where he supplied kayaks, camping gear, and anything for outdoor activities. Jeremiah's six-foot height, broad shoulders, and bearded face made him appear as a mountain man. His petite wife, Anna, worked alongside him. Zach said she had hiked the Appalachian Trail alone in her twenties. Jeremiah met her at one of the outposts when he and his buddies walked a section. Impressed with her ambition and determination, he had connected with her, and they'd married a few months later. She still led hikes on the trails and encouraged outdoor adventures.

With Jeremiah and Anna on hand, Zach and I had more time to roam the grounds and observe the people.

At ten o'clock, Aunt Cordy rang a bell to gather everyone's attention. Her white hair shimmered in the sunlight, as she stood on a small platform Walt had provided. Dressed in her soft blue sweatshirt with an apple tree embroidered on the front, she spoke. "Thank you so much for coming to the festival today. After last week, I wasn't sure whether to proceed, but I want to honor our town and our mayor, rest his soul. Let's take a moment of silence to remember him and all the work he did to improve Seldom Seen."

We all paused and bowed our heads. I opened my eyes and peered at the people. Otis stood with his arms crossed and stared at my aunt. Johnson Winters rested his hand on the table in Marcy Fox's booth. Mr. Garrison, with his red-feathered fedora in hand, bowed his head and moved his lips as if he prayed.

My aunt raised her head. "Thanks so much. I hope you enjoy the day and the apples."

With my camera in hand, I snapped photos of the petting zoo. The Valais Blacknose sheep were a hit. Kids and adults loved Floss and Thimble, and those fluffy girls loved every minute of attention. Bashful and Happy hopped about and jumped off and on the cable tables.

I watched Laurel hand out maps for all the activities. Her face would be tired from all the smiling. Beside the barn, Johnson Winters pointed out his handiwork to Otis. I snapped a couple of photos of them. They appeared chummy. I imagined Johnson had purchased supplies from Otis. The two of them hee-hawed at something. Good for them.

When I turned to check on Aunt Cordy, I ran into Mr. Garrison—with a jolt. My feet went out from under me, and I landed on my keister, on the wet ground where we had emptied a bucket of ice.

His baritone voice interrupted my embarrassment. "I'm so sorry. I didn't see you."

Fedora man held my arm and lifted me from the ground. He smiled, and tiny crinkles encased his emerald-green eyes. Once my feet held me in place, he let go. “I’m sorry. I wasn’t looking where I was going.” The wet ground had soaked my backside. Of all the places to fall, I had chosen the only place saturated with water.

“Are you okay?” Again, his deep voice rumbled in my ears.

I waved a hand in front of me. “I’m good. Wet, but no worse off than usual.”

“Is your camera okay? I’d hate for such a fine piece of equipment to be damaged.” He pointed at my camera.

Did he? Or did he want the photos on my camera ruined? Right now, I suspected him, but he may prove me wrong. “I’ve got to change my pants. Thanks for the hand.” I darted into the house. Inside, I ran up the steps to my room and changed into a clean pair of jeans. Before I ventured back to the festival, I sat on the bed and flipped through photos. Mr. Garrison stood in the background of several. It appeared he watched everyone and everything. Was he getting to know people? Or was he up to something else?

I rose from the bed and passed my window. Movement made me pause. From my perspective, I watched Otis and Johnson maneuver along the path to the river, where we had found the mayor’s body. Before I could stop myself, I flew down the steps and out the back door. Zach walked across the yard from the orchard, where he’d been sharing stories about how apples grow and of course, the great Johnny Appleseed. "Zach." A harsh whisper escaped my lips, and I waved him over.

"What's with the covert whispering?" Zach smoothed his hair off his face. Delight had called him cute. I'd say handsome, although he did have beautiful brown eyes like a Golden Retriever. Good grief. Focus.

I leaned into him. "I saw Otis and Johnson on the path leading to the old house foundation, where we discovered the mayor's body. Want to squirrel your way there with me?"

"Squirrel? Like hop from tree to tree." A gleam sparkled in those dark chocolate eyes.

I rolled my eyes. "Sort of. Sneak, tiptoe, whatever works."

We made our way along the edge of the tree-lined path. Hidden enough and close to the brush, we could duck if need be. We closed in on the old stone foundation and squatted behind a rhododendron, one of my favorite plants in the Appalachian Mountains. Voices rose above the flow of the river.

"No one will run against me for mayor now. I should win with no problem." I pictured Otis, thumbs under his suspenders, holding them out as his chest puffed with pride.

Johnson's voice sounded through the woods. "According to sources, the council elected Leo Randolph, the guy with the woodworking shop, as the temporary mayor. Why didn't they have you step in?"

"They have the option to change the pro-tem at every meeting. I'll have to talk to the other council members and see if I can step in."

"The new election isn't until next year, is it?" Johnson shuffled his feet in the leaves.

Through a space between branches, we spied on the men. Otis rubbed his boot in the dirt. "Wonder if they found any other clues to who did old Richardson in. I'm guessing he ticked somebody off."

Johnson stared at the river. "Not sure. Should we poke around and see if we find anything?"

"Nah. Let's head over and see if we left anything beside the campfire the other night. Cordy doesn't mind people fishing, but she don't want no messes." Zach and I watched them straggle off to the riverbank.

We stood and brushed leaves off of our pants. "They solved the campfire mystery. Men out fishing. Wouldn't you think they'd have doused the fire? It had burning shards when we found it. They could have started a forest fire." Zach raised his fist. His passion for the outdoors showed all over his face.

"For sure." I led the way back to the festival. "When did those two become friends?"

"I don't know, but I think you'd make a great mayor." Zach tapped my shoulder.

I stopped in my tracks and turned. "No thank you, sir. You'll have been here long enough to run. I'll campaign for you."

"Nope. I'll stick with the forest, thanks. What about your aunt?" Zach tossed a branch from the path into the woods.

We continued our ascent to the farm. "She's got her hands full, but Walt might run if we convince him." By the time we reached the Apple Fest, folks had filled every inch of space. Zach jogged to the orchard, and I moseyed along the main venue and snapped more photos. Aunt Cordy had loaded her table with another round of jellies and jams, apple butter, and one last cake. Her smile gleamed in the autumn sun. Although her large paddle was tied up in the investigation, she used a smaller pot and paddle over an open fire and demonstrated how pioneers made apple butter. She tossed chopped and peeled apples in the pot with water and stirred until they cooked down. She added sugar, cinnamon, and a pinch of nutmeg and let the mixture continue to cook while she stirred. The aroma of the apples and spices brought on my hunger pangs.

I wormed my way to the Gathering Place food truck and ordered a cheeseburger. The fries smelled good, but a girl can only eat so much. As predicted, the cheese dripped off the sides. I gathered pickles and a mayo packet from the side cart and sat at one of the tables we had set up earlier. I lifted my sandwich for a bite, and Marcy Fox came into my view. She carried a plate from the Early Bird Creperie.

"Care if I sit here?" Why did she want to sit with me?

"Have a seat." I took another bite.

She scooted onto the bench across from me. Her eyes, dressed in makeup and eyeliner, rounded. "I'm sorry about the other day."

"Um, thanks." With no idea what else to say, I sipped the water I'd grabbed from Aunt Cordy's booth.

"Seriously, I shouldn't have gotten so upset. The mayor blocked me from expanding, but he was my friend. We may have butted heads, but he did a lot for the town. My heart is broken. Who would kill him?" She cut into the crepe. Goat cheese oozed out with blueberries and walnuts, and she popped the bite into her mouth.

We both chewed. Ugh. How did I respond? I swallowed. "I'm sorry too. We'll all miss him."

"The rumor mill said we'll have almost a year of per-tem mayors. They can change the role at every town council meeting." She dabbed her mouth with her napkin. "I hope they find one person who can fill in, then maybe they'll run against Otis. He's too narrow-minded to serve as mayor." She stood, grabbed her plate and marched off. Talk about abrupt. She left half the crepe on her plate.

I popped my last bite into my mouth and closed my eyes. Then I heard a squeal. What on earth? I stood, tossed my garbage into a trash can and ran toward my aunt's booth.

Chapter Fourteen

The breeze stilled, and I sprinted. When I reached Aunt Cordy's booth, I planted both feet on the ground and balanced myself with my hands on her table. She stood with her hands on her head, staring at the table at the back of her booth.

"I can't find it." She bent over and rummaged through her supplies. An apple corer, a peeler, a small apple butter paddle, and a dishtowel landed on the ground.

I approached her and placed a hand on her back. "Aunt Cordy. What's wrong?" A group of gawkers surrounded us. She raised her face and met my line of vision. Her cheeks flushed red.

I turned to the crowd. "You all go enjoy the festival. We've got this under control." I shooed the people away, then took my aunt by her shoulders. "What is wrong?"

"It's gone."

"What's gone?"

Zach joined us. "Can I help?" The knight in shining armor arrived to save the day, or at least I hoped he could help with whatever happened.

"My apple butter paddle. The police have my biggest one, but now the next size down is missing. I finished my apple butter demonstration, washed the paddle, and placed it right there. She pointed at the table at the back of the booth. Do you suppose someone realized it made a good weapon, and they stole it?" Her mouth turned down into a sad frown.

"We'll search." I nodded my head toward the house. "Zack, you look in the kitchen, and I'll check through this stuff." I pointed at the booth's table and the boxes my aunt carried supplies in. "We'll find it."

With meticulous precision, I placed every piece of equipment, all the jars of apple products, and the other paraphernalia on the ground. No apple butter paddle appeared, except a small one she used on the stove in the kitchen.

Zach met me at the back of the booth. "I didn't find the paddle she described. She had a few small ones, but those are the ones she's collected for display. She showed them to me when I first moved here." He lowered his voice. "You don't think someone took it to..."

"No, Zach. I don't think there's a copycat. We need to search the grounds." I turned to my aunt. "Do you keep anything under the front table?" The red-checked tablecloth hanging to the ground hid the contents under the table.

"No, but you can check." She stepped aside, and I lifted the edge of the tablecloth. Nothing under there.

"We're going to walk around the festival and ask if anyone has seen it. I understand your panic after what happened last week, but we'll find it. Don't worry. Every worry steals some joy." I squeezed her shoulder.

"You're quoting my own words to me. Thank you." A small smile raised the corners of her lips.

Zach and I split up and wandered the grounds. I stopped in front of Marcy Fox's tent. "You haven't seen an apple butter paddle, have you? It's wooden and about two feet long and has a spatula-type end." She twisted in her canvas lawn chair and then stood.

She peered around her, then leaned into me. "Will someone else be whacked with it?" Her face paled.

I shook my head. "It's simply missing, and I'm trying to find it. Aunt Cordy uses her paddles when she makes her apple butter and applesauce. She had it out for her demonstration this morning." I patted her arm. "Keep an eye out. If it turns up, let me know."

Mr. Garrison approached us before my attempt to skedaddle. "Is something wrong?" Did his kind eyes mask a killer? And the fedora and feather. What was up with that?

A sigh escaped my lips, a sign of my impatience. He wanted to help and I needed to settle. "I'm trying to find my aunt's apple butter paddle." In detail, I described it to the man intent on helping.

"I'll keep an eye out." He turned and meandered off. Odd man.

After speaking to Otis, Jonquil, Anna, and Janine Oliver, owner of Read Past Bedtime, I found nothing. Not a clue. I ran into Zach at Rachel's flower booth. "Find anything?"

"Nope. Nothing." He banded his hair into a low ponytail. "The guy in the fedora asked me if I'd seen it."

"Yeah. I told him about it, and he's trying to help." I bit my lower lip. Where might it be? "Let's walk to the river. I hate to think about what we found last time, but it's worth a trip."

Zach followed me across the field, along the path to the old house foundation. An array of brown and scarlet leaves tumbled from the trees along the river. The sun shone through the branches, and the river sparkled like diamonds. A still calm rested where tragedy had struck. We climbed through the low opening and viewed the ground. Nothing. Nobody, thank goodness, and no paddle. However, something red caught my eye. I snapped a photo, then with a tissue, I picked up a red feather. Not one from a bird, but similar to the one Greg Garrison wore in his fedora. "What do you think of this, Zach?"

"We should give it to Danny. I saw him and Officer Ashton earlier." He stared at the feather. "The feather isn't from a cardinal or any other bird out here. It's manufactured."

I wrapped it in the tissue and tucked it into my pocket. "I want to ask Mr. Garrison myself before I involve Danny."

"What if he's the one who ended the mayor's life? Don't put yourself in danger." Those brown eyes bored into me.

"I'm already in too deep to worry about it. Let's head back." We jogged to the field, and I heard a thump. What on earth?

"I'm due back at the orchard." Zach ran across the field and disappeared into the grove of apple trees. I followed the thumping sound to the edge of the orchard. A young boy threw an apple he snatched from the ground to another boy, who held the apple butter paddle like a baseball bat. At the crack of the "bat" and unbelievable precision, the apple splattered. Their laughter shook the sky. I hated to interrupt their fun, but Aunt Cordy might lose her patience if the boys busted her paddle. Plus, they made a mess with the smashed apples. I wanted to save them from their parents. As I drew closer to them, they saw me, dropped the paddle and sprinted. They disappeared into the crowd before I caught them. I bent over laughing. When I got myself together, I examined the paddle and found no harm done.

I trekked to the house. In the kitchen, I ran warm water over the wood and cleaned the apple mush off. Aunt Cordy would enjoy the story of the apple butter paddle's adventure.

I carried the beauty out of the house and found my way to my aunt's booth. When she noticed me and what I held, she threw her arms in the air. "Hallelujah! You found it."

I placed it in her hands as if it were a scepter returned to the queen. I shared the story, and we laughed. "No doubt the Johnson boys. Just like their daddy and his brothers. Good boys, but ornery." She handed it back to me. "Would you take it to the house? I don't want it to disappear again. It belonged to my great-grandmother."

"Of course." On my way inside, I spied Greg Garrison at Whittler's Woodworking, where Leo Randolph displayed his handmade items. The talented woodworker created the most beautiful Santas carved and painted in a variety of colors. He attached a tag to tell which country each St. Nicholas represented. My aunt owned one of his Santas dressed in a green robe similar to the version sometimes depicted in England. Before I forgot, I slipped the paddle into the kitchen and then hurried outside to try to catch Mr. Fedora.

Back in the sunshine, I hurried to Leo's booth, but the man I wanted to speak to had left.

"Hi, Lyndie." Leo's employee greeted me. In his twenties, he attended one of the local colleges.

"Hey. How are you?" I searched for Mr. Garrison in the crowd.

"I'm good. Looking for someone?"

"I'm sorry, and yes. I wanted to speak to the gentleman in the fedora." I scrunched my nose and cringed with apology.

He pointed to the Gathering Place food truck. "He mentioned how good the burgers smelled. Maybe he's over there."

"Thank you." I waved and marched to the food trucks. Sure enough, the man I planned to confront sat at a table alone. Before I plopped myself across from him, Johnson Winters balanced a basket with a burger and fries and his drink and sat at the table. *Oh, bother.* One of my favorite character's sayings. I wish I had the Pooh Bear my aunt had gifted me with on my eighth birthday to hug right now. The fuzzy—kind of ratty—old bear brought me comfort when I lived in Guatemala. He reminded me my aunt prayed for Laurel and me every day. Now he lived on the shelf beside my bed.

Without much consideration, I purchased a cupcake from Baker's Delight and planted myself at the table behind the two men. One of the best skills I'd learned during my time in the war fields was pretend to be invisible and listen with intent. Delight's cupcake melted in my mouth. Apple, caramel, and pecan lit my taste buds. Yum.

Johnson Winters' voice amplified from the table behind me. "Mr. Garrison, what brought you to Seldom Seen?"

The man cleared his throat. "You might say the north winds blew me here." A slurping sound followed his statement.

"You from the New England states or something?" Winters took a bite and chewed out loud. Gross.

"Something. What about you? I hear you've been here for a few months. What brought you to the most beautiful place on earth?"

"I'm not sure your description is accurate, although I enjoy the mountains." He slurped his drink. *Could he be any louder?* "I had some business here to take care of, and I decided to stay for a while. The work is good. Everyone needs something fixed, and I've made a few good friends." He paused. "If we stay long enough, we could run for mayor." He hee-hawed.

Mr. Garrison let out a deep laugh. "I'm not mayor material. Too much stress."

The two men bid each other a see you around, cleared their table and left. I kept an eye on the fedora as it bobbed above the crowd. Without drawing attention to myself, I moved through the people and followed him to the porta-potties on the edge of the driveway. Awkward, but I waited, about three yards away.

When he exited, I called his name.

"Miss Lavender." He tipped his hat. A full head of blond hair covered his head. He leveled the fedora on his head and stood beside me. Had we formally met? I hadn't known his name until Danny told me, but he knew mine.

Words failed me until I poked my hand into my pocket and found the tissue. "Are you enjoying the festival?"

"Very much so. How about you? I imagine this is a great deal of work for you and your aunt." He motioned to the main thoroughfare.

"It is, but we enjoy it." I tugged the tissue from my pants pocket. The red feather he wore in his hat sat in place, so where did this one come from? "Um." I unwrapped the feather. "I found this and wondered if it was yours, but you still have one."

He lifted the feather from the covering. "It may be. I noticed mine went missing, but I had another to replace it with. I keep a bag of them. You see, when I was a boy, my grandfather wore a similar hat." He removed it from his head. "He tucked a red feather in it to remind him to show love to others. He said the red represented his heart. The very heart he'd given to my grandmother, who passed at a young age. Grandfather was a sentimental chap. My mom said I took after him." He turned the feather in his hands. "I appreciate you thinking of me."

"You're welcome. I'd noticed your hat and couldn't miss the feather, but tell me, why were you down by the river?"

Chapter Fifteen

Thank goodness a slight breeze kept the noxious odor of the porta-potties at bay. Mr. Garrison and I matched steps as we wandered away from the driveway and moved toward the booths. He fingered the feather I had given him, and I searched for Danny, in case I needed him.

"The river." My walking companion furrowed his brow. "I must confess..."

Here goes. Was he going to tell me he'd hit the mayor with the apple butter paddle and left him to die? Then, he had returned to the scene of the crime.

He removed his fedora and played with the brim. "I must confess, I hiked to the river to see where our mayor lost his life. When I arrived, I sat on the rock wall. In contemplation, I removed my hat and bowed my head. I prayed for the person who killed him and for the police officers who are working to capture him or her." His eyes watered. "I arrived in town not long ago, but I saw the mayor had done a fine job creating a safe place, a town where people thrived. Then to have his life cut short broke my heart." He placed his hand on my arm. "Please keep this to yourself. I am a private person and prefer not to get tangled in town politics or gossip."

My heart sank to my toes. How could I have accused this kind man of such a cruel crime? His sincerity flowed through his words and expressions. Serenity covered his face. I'd mark him off my list. "Thank you for sharing, and I'm sorry."

"Sorry?"

"Yes, I had you on a list of suspects, and now I'll mark you off." I huffed.

Mr. Garrison leaned back and laughed. "I've never been on a list of that sort. So glad you can take me off." He pushed his fedora onto his head. "Thank you for clearing me. You are a delight, Lyndie. I hope to chat with you again soon."

He sauntered off, and I stood there frozen to the ground. I'd accused an innocent man of murder. Not merely innocent, but also kind and concerned. Still, I questioned why he had come to Seldom Seen. Why did anyone stop here and stay for a while? I did because of my family connection, but why did others? Another mystery for another time.

Eliminating Aunt Cordy and Greg Garrison left four suspects on my list: Otis Reardon, Marcy Fox, Johnson Winters, and June Bower. Their motives seemed clear. Otis coveted the mayor's office. Marcy wanted to expand her business, but the mayor had stood in her way. Johnson Winters...well, I wasn't sure of his motive, but he certainly reeked of suspicion and appeared in cahoots with Marcy. Then, of course, the mayor had fired June. Where was June today? I hadn't seen her since last week, when she had a breakdown at the gate.

I checked my watch. Two o'clock already. The day had passed like some days in the war zone—fast. Other days had dragged, but most zoomed by because we worked to stay alive even as we captured the heartbreaking news. The day my beloved, Elias, lost his life proved the longest day in my history. I had clung to Psalm 34:18, "The Lord is close to the brokenhearted..." Were folks who had been friends with the mayor clinging to the verse too? Danny had searched for family but found no one. One time Laurel heard the mayor refer to an ex-wife, but no one confirmed.

Before I grew roots in the dirt I stood on, I strode to my aunt's booth. She smiled at a customer and handed her the last apple cake and a box of apple muffins. In her element, she appeared ten years younger than her sixty-something age. I had feared the stress of the mayor's demise and the overwhelming preparation of the festival might weigh her down, but she flourished when she shared about her well-loved apple orchard and the produce she harvested. I snapped a few photos, then wandered to the petting zoo. Our neighbor, Ashley, had brought three of her black and white Rex rabbits. Three kiddos sat on the ground with a bunny in each of their laps. One boy I had caught with the apple butter paddle earlier petted his bunny and whispered to it. The calm of placing a hand on soft fur drove me to my sheep.

Floss and Thimble skipped to me. They raised their pretty black faces, and I believe they smiled at me. Oh, how I needed these beauties in my life. I scrunched the fleece on Floss, and she pushed closer to me. What if I were a sheep? I'd be fed and watered and live a life of leisure until some wolf broke through the fence and devoured me. A soft breeze pulled me back into reality and the beauty around me. I patted Floss's head, then wandered over to find Laurel.

A few people chatted with her as she pointed and offered directions around the homestead. I photographed her bright smile and captured her pleasant personality. She loved helping people.

"Hey, Sister." She waved to me as I approached her.

"Hi. How's your day going? It's close to three o'clock. Two more hours until we close for the day."

She straightened the pamphlets on her table. "The day has gone amazingly well. Many of the visitors are from out of town and weren't around last weekend, so I didn't get bombarded with questions about the mayor's death. People have inquired about my website and taken my business card. I may get some more business from nearby towns."

"Wonderful." I propped my camera on a chair and rubbed my neck. "Sometimes I forget how heavy my equipment is." I leaned close to her. "I had an interesting chat with Greg Garrison. He's different, but he's got a kind heart. I'm still not sure why he's in Seldom Seen, but it's not my business."

"So, we're down to four?" Laurel squinted her eyes. The sun shone brighter than it had all day. Should I take this as a sign of hope we'd solve the mayor's murder or, rather, that Danny and the police would?

"Have you talked to your hubby today? I saw him and Officer Ashton at the food trucks earlier, but I didn't have time to talk to them." I had been too busy eavesdropping on Mr. Garrison and Johnson Winters, but I didn't tell Laurel.

"He stopped by when he got here, but I haven't seen him since. He wanted to see if June showed up today, but I haven't seen her."

"Neither have I." I hit my forehead with my palm. "I forgot to tell you. Marcy Fox apologized to me for being so angry. If she's a legitimate suspect, she's buttering me up, or she's sincere. I can't decide. She claimed she and the mayor were friends, and she's devastated by his death, but she didn't act that way when it happened."

"Marcy was always emotional in school. The time I made the cheerleading squad instead of her, you'd have thought I'd committed a crime. She wailed in the locker room, then told everyone I didn't deserve it because I couldn't do the splits." Laurel's hands rested on her hips. "I could do the splits, and I showed her."

"I remember. You did them every time one of the players made a basket. I was afraid you'd break yourself." I tried to hold back a laugh but failed. Laurel glared at me. "Sorry."

"Sure, you are." She tapped the edges of her pamphlets to straighten them. "One thing I don't understand is why Marcy is hanging out with Johnson Winters. He's at least fifteen years older than her."

"Maybe she's lonely, and he paid attention to her."

My sister shrugged, then stood on her toes and peered over my shoulder. "There's Danny. He's coming our way."

My brother-in-law kissed Laurel on the cheek. "Hello, ladies."

The smile on his face encouraged me to draw from my well of courage. "So, have you uncovered any clues today?"

The smile on his face dropped to a frown. "Lyndie, I was having a good day. Nothing bad happening, and then you have to go and pry." He tilted his head and gave me his look. My gut said I had crossed the proverbial line.

With a hand on one hip, I lifted my chin. "I want to help."

He crossed his arms across his chest. "Then you tell me what you've learned." The dare hung between us. Did I spill or forget it?

I stepped closer to him to speak in a quiet voice. "Johnson Winters appears to be in cahoots with Marcy Fox, who was angry with the mayor over him blocking her expansion. Greg Garrison is innocent." I explained what I'd learned from the mysterious visitor. "Winters suggested he or Mr. Garrison run for mayor next year."

Danny narrowed his gaze. "Did they tell you that?"

"Not exactly. They chatted at lunch, and I happened to sit behind them." Not a total fib.

Danny blew out a breath. "You eavesdropped, didn't you? I don't want anyone mixed up in the investigation. You survived war, but someone killed the mayor, whether by accident or on purpose. You don't need to be next."

"I'm sorry, but I'm concerned. It happened on Aunt Cordy's land." We stood facing one another with our arms crossed.

"I can't stop you, but don't drag Laurel into your little investigation." He stared at my sister. She raised her hand in front of her and backed further into her booth. There went one of my helpers.

"Laurel, I'll see you at home this evening. Officer Ashton is staying here. I've got to head to the office." He gave her a quick kiss. "Love you." Then he stalked off.

I wrapped my camera's strap around my neck. "Sorry, Laurel. I didn't mean to cause trouble, but I want to solve the mayor's murder. Of course, the police are doing their job. I don't doubt for a minute, but there's something in me that drives me to seek the truth. You understand, right?" Uncertain I understood myself, I longed for more than farm work. The past six months I'd found rest and peace and I wanted to continue to help Aunt Cordy, but my restless spirit needed a challenge. Why not use my skills to solve a murder?

"You've been curious since you first walked and talked. What else would push someone to put themselves in danger for twenty years and leave your family wondering every day if we'd get a phone call we didn't want? You've stood for truth since college. I love you and appreciate your drive, and I'm thankful you respect Danny and the other police officers, but please be careful. I have something to share, but I can't right now. There is a customer approaching." She hugged me.

I lifted and waved the camera. "I'd better take the rest of the photos you wanted."

At the Read Past Your Bedtime booth, Janine read aloud to a group of children. She performed various voices, and the characters jumped off the page. I snapped several photos. My mom had read to Laurel and me every night before bed. Her calm voice poured comfort over us before we fell into slumber. I missed Mom and Dad, but they lived their own lives and fulfilled their calling as I had. I couldn't begrudge them for helping others. When I considered leaving my job, I had prayed about joining them but living with Aunt Cordy made more sense for me. Thankful for my choice, I embraced the people of Seldom Seen and longed to help in any possible way.

By four o'clock, I had taken advantage of the lighting and snapped at least one hundred photos of the folks enjoying the festival. One more hour and we'd wrap up the day. The crowd had thinned when I heard someone yell. The voice drew me to Marcy Fox's booth. June stood in front of Marcy with her niece, Luna. "What do you mean, you don't want Luna to paint your new sign? Why not?"

Marcy held on to her table. Her knuckles turned white. "I've decided to have Genevieve paint it for me. She needs the job."

"So does Luna." June's voice rose.

Luna held her aunt's arm and tugged her away from the booth. "It's okay, Aunt June. I'm fine with Genevieve doing the job. I've got a couple of mural paintings to complete in town."

June muttered to herself, jerked her arm away, then stalked off, while Luna stood and watched.

"Luna, are you okay?"

She swung toward me. "Yeah. Aunt June hasn't been the same since the mayor let her go. She loved her job, but the guilt of letting him down eats at her. I wish she'd find something else to do. Working with Otis hasn't been good for her. He's so negative."

No doubt.

Chapter Sixteen

The late afternoon sun cast shadows across the festival, as a cool breeze lifted leaves from the ground into a whirl of autumn color. Vendors packed their wares and closed their booths. I hiked to the house to put my camera away before I helped Aunt Cordy. As I stepped onto the porch, a flash of movement caught my eye. I followed the movement around the corner of the house. Someone hustled toward the field.

Without hesitation, I followed. Maybe not the smartest move, but I couldn't stop myself. In the distance, a short, gray-haired person tramped through the yellowed grass, dressed in a blue plaid flannel shirt. June. What was she doing trotting to the river?

I hustled through the dried grass. My lungs were out of breath by the time I reached the edge of the woods, beside the water. I treaded along the path, my curiosity at its peak. June beat her fists on the low wall. She sobbed. Not sure what to do, I observed. No one else joined her as she poured out her sorrow. From along the river's edge, a figure emerged from the trees. *What's he doing here?*

Leo Randolph must have closed his booth and followed June too. I ducked behind a bush.

"June." He opened his arms, and she walked into them. She sobbed, and he patted her back. After a few minutes, June's shoulders stopped shaking, and she leaned away from Leo.

"Did you follow me?" She pulled further away from him.

He ran his hand through his comb-over. "I'm worried about you, Juney. You haven't been yourself for a while. Luna told me you blame yourself for the mayor's death. Unless you hit him with the paddle, I don't see how that's possible."

This was it. A confession. Instead, June shoved Leo away. "I told you not to call me Juney. My husband called me by my nickname, and no one else did. I'm fine. Leave me alone and stop talking to Luna. She has no idea what she's talking about." She jerked away from him and dashed to the field. Dashed might be an exaggeration, but she hurried past me without seeing me.

Leo leaned against the broken-down wall. I wandered out of my hiding place and stepped in front of him. "Hey."

"Hi, Lyndie. What are you doing here?"

"I live here. My question is, what have you learned about June and her involvement in the mayor's death?" My voice held confidence while my legs shook.

He stood away from the wall. "I don't know anything except she's upset. I suppose you saw her reject my help." The odor of dead leaves whirled around us as the wind kicked up.

"Did you have anything to do with the mayor's demise? You're the pro-tem now."

"Of course not. If it were up to me, I'd not be in this position, but they voted. Next month, we'll pick someone else. And how do I know you didn't do it? You'd best be careful who you accuse." He turned and stalked away. My mouth flew open.

Zach approached from the wooded area where I had hidden. "You'd better close your mouth, so the bugs don't get in."

"So, you overheard Leo." I rested my behind against the wall.

Zach joined me. "Yeah. He sounded heated. June darted past me through the yard to her car, and she and Luna peeled out on their way down the driveway. June drove." He chuckled.

I pushed myself off from the wall, moss soft under my hands. "Something is going on with June. She sobbed, then yelled at Leo."

"She appeared tense the last time I shopped at the hardware store." Zach glanced at the sky. "The sun's about to set. Want to head back?"

"Sure." I trailed behind Zach. A flock of geese sailed overhead in a V and honked a greeting. I fingered the button on my camera. My conscience had kept me from photographing June in her personal moment. Even I had limits, but I wished I had confronted her. She may have explained why she felt at fault for the mayor's death. Yet, I hadn't. I'd track her down this week and chat with her.

By the time we reached the house, my shoulders relaxed. We found Aunt Cordy, Laurel, and Walt in the kitchen. Laurel sliced and served triangles of apple pie Aunt Cordy had made. The cinnamon and apple smell made my tongue tingle. She placed slices for Zach and me at the empty seats, so we slid into the chairs and joined them.

One bite and my taste buds danced. The sweet and tart flavor almost let the day float away, but I had news to report. I swallowed a drink of tea, then cleared my throat. "Did anyone else see June today?"

Walt rested his fork on the pie plate. "About four-thirty, she wandered into the yard. Luna stopped at the Baa Baa Black Sheep booth, but June hustled past me. I watched her meet Otis behind his booth, and the two of them put their heads together and conversed. At one point, she leaned away from him and yelled. 'I didn't do it.' Then she ran off."

I pushed a piece of crust around with my fork. "I followed her to the river. Leo was there too. She cried, and it sounded like she blamed herself for the mayor's death. Leo tried to comfort her, but she ran from him. Have the two of them been close?"

Laurel harrumphed. "Leo has been chasing after June for years. She deflected his advances. She'd moved here after her husband's death. They'd lived away, but she wanted to come to Seldom Seen to live near his family, since she didn't have any of her own. She took care of herself until she messed up with the mural debacle."

I shoved my plate away. "What I saw was a woman who needed help."

Laurel gathered the empty plates and deposited them into the sink, then sat at the table. "By the way, Danny and Officer Ashton discussed alibis earlier today." She glanced at me. "They stood too close to my tent." A grin crossed her face. "So far, the only people with a solid alibi for the time of the murder are Aunt Cordy—I mean her alibi is Danny—and Greg Garrison. They said Otis waffled about where he was, and Johnson Winters and Marcy used each other, which doesn't hold water. He didn't mention June, but I'm not sure if they are considering her as a serious suspect."

I watched my sister's animation as she spoke. "You told Danny you'd keep out of the investigation."

She twitched her mouth. "I'm not getting involved. I'm sharing information." She crossed her arms over her chest.

Everyone at the table chuckled.

By nine o'clock, I climbed the steps to my room. Everyone else had dispersed, and I needed some peace and quiet. Per my usual nighttime routine, I clicked through the photos from the festival. Those sweet sheep of mine stood inside their fence while children and adults petted them. I imagined the coos the people whispered to them. The goats played with a little boy who chased them along the fence. They had romped back and forth for a while. Laurel beamed at me from her booth, and her dark hair gleamed in the sunlight. I caught Leo carving with his knife as folks gathered to watch him turn a hunk of wood into a miniature golden retriever.

Wait, a minute. June and Luna's faces, intent on Leo, frowned. My camera reported the timestamp as three o'clock. They'd been on the grounds earlier in the afternoon. Why hadn't I seen June then? The next photo showed Mr. Garrison purchasing a hank of yarn from Jonquil. My favorite photo of the day, besides my sheep, had to be Read Past Your Bedtime. The children sat mesmerized as Janine read them a story. I wanted to stop at her shop next week and pick up the next Kim Garee book. Perhaps Janine had noticed something at the festival the week before. I hadn't asked her. The sweet, quiet bookstore owner kept to herself, unless she found the opportunity to talk about books. She had a superpower for matching people with the right story.

Before I laid my head on the pillow, I opened my Bible and read the twenty-third Psalm. Even if I walked through the valley of death, I'd fear no evil. David must have been one brave soul. From now on, I'd press this into my heart and figure out what happened. God's peace calmed me as I drifted off to sleep.

Sunday morning after church, my aunt, Zach, and I hurried home to set up for the afternoon festivities we didn't get to do the previous Sunday. Zach had planned a hayride, and I volunteered for a photo booth with the animals. As I pulled my Jeep into the driveway, June's car blocked me. She stood on the gravel with her hands on her hips.

Now what?

Zach had parked behind me in his truck. I climbed out of my car and left my aunt inside. "Hey, June. Can I help you?"

"You can mind your own business." She stomped her foot.

With small hesitant steps, I moved away in case she tried to swing at me. "What do you mean?"

"Leo told me you spied on me yesterday at the river. I needed to let my emotions out. Without an audience."

My eyes locked with hers. "I'm sorry. I wasn't trying to spy, and I didn't want to interrupt you or bother you. So, I stayed hidden." Not to mention, I was nosy. I respected her privacy, but if she had something to do with the mayor's demise, I wanted to find out.

"Leave me alone. I cared about the mayor. He was my friend." Tears poured down her face again.

I approached her and wrapped an arm around her shoulders. "I understand, but you said his death was your fault." I'd stepped in the proverbial mud now.

Her shoulders stopped shaking. "I had spoken to him before he walked to the river. We had some words I'm not proud of. I hate working for Otis. He belittles me and thinks he can demand me to do things I don't want to do."

"What kind of things?" Afraid she'd stepped into a mess working for Otis, I wanted to help her.

Her eyes studied my face. "Lift heavy boxes, move equipment, set up displays I can't lift, and work late. I'm not young or used to physical labor, plus he smells bad. The cigar smoke and sweaty odor make me sick. I complained to Mayor Richardson, and he refused to hire me back. He had filled my position, and he didn't trust me. Yeah, he shouldn't have, but I was desperate. I yelled at him, and he retreated to the river. If I hadn't yelled, he'd still be alive."

From the corner of my eye, I saw Zach. Good, he heard what she said. "He may have walked to the river anyway. You don't know. He often stopped by and visited the old foundation where the homestead stood. Aunt Cordy said he loved the quiet. I'm betting he would have gone to the river whether you yelled at him or not." I placed a hand on each of her shoulders and leaned down to look her in the eyes. "Come to the house and have lunch with us. We're going to prepare for the rest of the day's festivities."

"I shouldn't. I don't want to bother you."

"You aren't a bother. We'd love for you to join us." I guided her to her car.

"Okay." She climbed into her Yaris, and we followed her up the driveway.

With our cars tucked away behind the barn, we ambled to the house. Aunt Cordy hugged June to her side. "I understand June. I lost the love of my life, and it's not easy. We'll try to help you find another job." My aunt had her window down during the conversation and had listened to our exchange, and in Aunt Cordy fashion, she would find June what she needed.

Chapter Seventeen

By two in the afternoon, festivalgoers milled around the field. The sun sparkled with the promise of a beautiful day. I climbed onto the wagon for the first round of hayrides. Zach steered the tractor away from the festivities and toward the pasture. Adults and children jostled, as the tractor bumped along. About halfway through the ride, one of the moms started singing, and everyone joined in.

Zach drove along the bank of the river, as I watched the water rush past and disappear around a curve. As a child, Laurel and I played near the water, never too close, but we would toss sticks in and watch them float away. The power of the water fascinated me now, but as a child, I had not understood the danger. Was the danger the mayor encountered expected, or had he been surprised? Danny let it slip that the apple butter paddle left a knot on Mayor Richardson's head. They surmised he fell on a sharp piece of the foundation's rubble, which cut into his neck and sliced the carotid artery. How awful. Even if his death appeared an accident, he had angered someone, and they took revenge. With time on my hands, I had to figure out who the someone was.

The wagon turned toward the house and the festival. While the other folks sang, I considered our lunch with June. Aunt Cordy had served roast beef, carrots, potatoes, and tomatoes she had prepped in the crock pot, one of my favorite meals. When we walked into the kitchen, the fragrance of warm comfort food spiced with garlic met our noses. At first, June had picked at her food, but my aunt found a way of making people comfortable, no matter the circumstances. She had asked June about Luna's art. June loved to brag about her niece. Once the conversation steered in Luna's direction, June couldn't stop talking, until she did. She squinted her eyes and stared at me.

"What's wrong?" I tilted my head and waited for an answer.

"You're trying to figure out who killed the mayor, aren't you?"

I pushed from the table and crossed my legs. "Kind of."

She leaned toward me. "I hope you are. We need to solve this as soon as we can."

"Have you learned something that might help?" Not sure what to say to her when she said *we*, I attempted to find out if she had insider information.

"You can't trust Otis. He's a two-faced liar."

Not certain if her comment came from anger at him for making her work hard or if she believed he lied. "If you hear anything from him which implies he may have been involved, will you tell me?"

"You bet I will." The fire returned to her eyes.

The wagon rolled to a stop, and my daydreaming ended. I jumped off and jogged to check on Aunt Cordy. Before I reached her, Greg Garrison stopped me. "Lyndie, can we talk for a moment?"

"Sure." The man, still a mystery to me, moved away from the bustle of people.

I followed him to a spot behind the booths, away from listening ears. My curiosity revved.

He glanced around and then faced me. "I heard something in town this morning you may be interested in. I understand you're trying to figure out who killed the mayor."

Did everyone know? Of course, I had spoken to him about where he had been the day the mayor died. "I'm happy to listen to anything you think might be of interest." By the time I finished my sentence, two children dashed past me, and I lost my balance. My bottom landed on the ground.

Mr. Garrison reached for my hand and helped me stand. I brushed off my jeans. "Goodness. Thanks for the hand up. I'm not usually this clumsy." *Could I be any more klutzy, falling in front of him twice.* Good thing he seemed like a kind man.

"Kids need to be more aware of their surroundings. When I taught, I tried to instill some respect in my students."

Aha. One piece of Mr. G's past. No surprise he had taught school. His formal speech made me suspect he might have been a professor.

"Anyway, as I was saying. I visited the hardware store before I returned to the festival. The screen door on the cottage where

I'm staying needed a spring, so I told Mrs. Rawlins I'd repair it for her. She's been so kind to me and often delivers dinner. She says she doesn't enjoy cooking for one, so she wants to share." He took a breath. "The hardware was open today, which surprised me since it's Sunday, but when I saw the open sign, I stopped." He scooted closer to me and looked around again. "When I stepped inside, Otis's loud voice met me. He spoke to a woman with blond hair. She has a booth here and owns one of the stores in town. She shuddered when he told her he planned to run for mayor and take over the town. He wants to change the name of the town to Reardonville." His eyebrows raised.

"Sounds like Otis."

"Then he told her if she told anyone, he'd make sure the town knew her secret." Mr. Garrison removed his hat and ran his hand through his hair. "I'm not one for gossip, but with the mystery of the mayor's death and the possibility of a killer still lurking, I'm concerned. You are the most trustworthy person I've met here."

I watched relief wash over his face. "Thank you for sharing. I appreciate your trust." I adjusted my glasses on my nose. "Will you be staying much longer?" He appeared trustworthy too, while secretive about himself.

"I'm not certain. Your town is lovely, but I want to figure out some things in my life first. I'm here to rest and relax and decide on my next steps in this glorious life."

I understood. “Enjoy the rest of the festival. If you haven’t purchased my aunt’s apple butter, you should. It’s delicious. And some homemade bread from Delight.”

“I believe I will. Thank you.” He sauntered off to the booths.

Before I moved on, Zach touched my elbow, and I jumped. “Are you part ninja?”

“Sorry, I didn’t mean to startle you. What’s going on with Mr. Garrison?” Zach brushed a piece of straw from his jeans.

I relayed what the mystery man had told me about Otis’s desire to take over the town. He’d upend the progress Mayor Richardson had achieved and build Seldom Seen into his little kingdom.

Zach’s eyes grew round. “Someone has to run against him. Have you talked to Walt? Would he be wiling?”

“Want to see if we can find him?” I waved my hand, and Zach followed me to the midway of the festival. Before we searched for Walt, I stopped beside Marcy Fox’s booth. The blond at Otis’s hardware store fit her description. Mr. Garrison hadn’t met all the shop owners. He hung out at Baker’s Delight. I mean, who wouldn’t? Her baked goods pleased the taste buds like no other. The sour-cherry scones she baked melted in my mouth.

Johnson Winters sidled up to the booth. I motioned for Zach to back behind the booth with me. We stood in silence and waited for a conversation to ensue. Sure enough, Johnson’s voice drifted to us.

"Have you heard anything about the investigation into the mayor's death? The police aren't getting any closer to finding the culprit." He cleared his throat.

Marcy's voice purred. Ugh. I pictured her placing her hand on his. "No. I haven't, but I'm not worried about it. We gave an alibi for each other. Besides, I didn't do it. However, we need to find someone else to run for mayor besides Otis. The man is crazy."

Zach tapped my shoulder, and I turned to face him. "Don't they understand they can't alibi each other?"

"Pretty sure they have no idea." Zach stood in front of me, close enough I noticed his long eyelashes over his dark brown eyes. Nope, I can't go there. Yes, he's handsome and my age. He's kind-hearted and caring. Nope. No time for attraction. Focus on solving the murder and helping my aunt. Besides, my grief over Elias's death had left a crack in my heart.

"Let's see if we can find Walt." I turned and headed to the main thoroughfare.

Zach hustled to my side. "He's over there at Laurel's booth."

We speedwalked to catch him. At the Seldom Seen booth, I smacked my hands on Laurel's table to stop myself from falling on her and to get their attention. "Hey, Walt. Can we chat for a moment?"

Laurel parked a hand on each hip and frowned. "Lyndie, didn't Mom and Dad teach you manners too?"

"Sorry, Sis. I need to speak to Walt." I made the please can I look I had used on my parents when we were children.

She gave me the same look Mom had, which translated to *seriously*?

Walt eyed me, then Laurel. "You two don't need to fight over me. I'm happy to chat with both of you." His cheeks pinked.

I scooted closer to Walt, as did Zach. My sister stared at me. "You can hear this too, Laurel, but no one else can." I locked eyes with Walt. "We want you to run for mayor."

The man stepped back from me, his mouth open, but no words coming out. He scrubbed his hand across his forehead. "Why?"

I glanced at Zach, and he took the hint. "Lyndie and I have learned a certain man in town has the intention of gaining the mayorship and taking over Seldom Seen, even to the point of changing the name to Reardonville."

Walt's expression changed to one of horror. His eyes widened, and his cheeks reddened. "Oh, no. We can't let him take control of our town, but I'm not mayor material."

I stepped closer and touched the sleeve of his plaid flannel shirt. "You ran a business for thirty-five years and left it in good stead with your son. Your leadership skills shine at church. We can't let Otis win."

Walt held his hand out in front of him. "Slow down. The election is almost a year away. Perhaps another candidate will step forward. I'm too old to run and do the job justice. Plus, I want to enjoy your aunt's company without being burdened by a job. Retirement calls my name." He lowered his hand. "We'll put our heads together and come up with someone who will be willing to do the job and want the position. Until then, let's weigh the options." He turned to Laurel. "How about you?"

She stood from the wooden folding chair. "No thank you. I'm busy enough with my kids and job, plus Danny would work for me. Nope. Not happening, but I'm sure there's someone who might want to continue the improvements of our sweet little town. If the name changed, I'd cry. And not just because my blog, *Come See What's in Seldom Seen*, would be a bust. I'll keep my eyes and ears tuned in. I've met most of our residents or someone related to them. Perhaps the position of mayor will interest one of our younger community members." She tapped her finger on her mouth.

Before I thanked Walt for listening, he darted off. I kept him in my line of sight and watched him confront a man at Aunt Cordy's booth. What on earth was happening? Calm and collected Walt fisted his hands and stood toe-to-toe with a white-haired man.

Zach, Laurel, and I bolted to the booth. Aunt Cordy tugged on Walt's sleeve. "You two stop. I'll not have any nonsense at my festival." She wedged herself between them, and they broke apart. The man stalked off toward the parked cars. I kept my eye on him until he climbed into a red pickup truck and drove off.

"Walt, he wasn't bothering me. He has in the past, but he simply asked how I was. He meant no harm." Aunt Cordy held both of Walt's hands.

The folks who had watched the interaction dispersed, except for June. When did she show up?

She grasped my aunt's arm. "Are you okay?"

Aunt Cordy let go of Walt's hands and turned to June. "I'm fine. There was a small misunderstanding. Don't you worry after me, June."

June hugged my aunt and left.

Laurel and I wrapped Aunt Cordy in a group hug. I let go and stepped back. "Who was he?"

Chapter Eighteen

Many of the visitors waved at Aunt Cordy as they guided their families to their vehicles. The crowd had thinned, and the time neared four-thirty. The festival closed in half an hour. My shoulders ached where I held my stress, and my feet hurt, but the long weekend had blessed me.

Zach, Laurel, and I waited with Walt and my aunt until most of the patrons had left. A few lingered over Baa Baa Black Sheep's hand-spun yarn and Read Past Bedtime's books. Once no one stood near us, I faced my aunt. "Who was the white-haired man?"

Aunt Cordy sorted the apple products left in her inventory into boxes. Most had sold, so she didn't have much to store. She ran a finger around the top of an apple butter jar, then she raised her head to us, and her eyes watered. "He's the man I almost married instead of your uncle. Last year he found me. He had lived in Charleston when I did, and we dated for about a year. Before the year ended, I had met your uncle. I broke up with Jenson, the man you saw, and it angered him. He had a temper and threatened me. Your uncle protected me and, as you know, we moved to Seldom Seen." She dabbed her eyes with a tissue.

"I'm not sure why I'm all emotional, except it's been a long day. Anyway, he found me last year and stopped to see me when Walt was here. He apologized and wanted to stay in touch, but I didn't know him anymore and wanted nothing to do with him. I told Walt the whole story."

"I'd never let anyone hurt you." He hugged Aunt Cordy's shoulders.

"Jenson stopped by today to tell me he moved to Greenville. I'm not thrilled about it, but I can't stop him. Walt told him not to bother me, and I think he got the message." She kissed Walt on the cheek. "Thank you."

Pink colored Walt's cheeks again. What a sweet man. Too bad he didn't want to run for mayor.

Zach stepped beside Aunt Cordy. "If he causes you any trouble, call me. If I'm at the cabin, I'm not far away."

"I will." She patted his arm. "Let's get these boxes inside." She raised her head and glanced at the other vendors. "Everyone is packing to go home. Let me speak to them on their way out." She made her way to the end of the booths and chatted with vendors as they left. My aunt amazed me. She worked circles around me and kept the most positive attitude. My heart swelled when I watched Walt stack and carry her boxes into the house. He'd protect her and keep her out of harm's way. Thank goodness Jenson left. I hoped he'd stay gone.

Laurel closed her booth and packed her boxes, while I checked on the animals. The ones borrowed from other farms had left with their owners. Thimble and Floss chomped on the food I'd deposited into their trough, and Murphy trotted beside me while I carried water to his bowl. They all appeared as ready for bed as I was. I freshened the straw in the sheep's shed and patted them good night. Happy and Bashful danced around my feet while I prepped their pen for the night. In Pakistan, I had the privilege of helping a family with their goats. An international agriculture group had gifted them with two, which developed into a small herd. The woman of the household worked hard to nurture her small herd and create a small business selling the milk and some of the goats. She had left an impression on me to never be afraid of hard work.

By six thirty, Laurel had rounded up my niece and nephew and driven them home. Aunt Cordy, Walt, Zach, and I shared dinner in the kitchen. After a long day, ham and cheese sandwiches, fresh veggies, and lemonade pleased my palate. For dessert, Walt sliced into a white coconut cake he'd purchased from Baker's Delight. The sweetness of the coconut flakes filled my mouth with joy and reminded me of the fresh coconut I'd eaten in Sri Lanka.

Walt pushed his empty dessert plate to the middle of the table. "Did Lyndie tell you she wanted me to run for mayor?"

"No." Aunt Cordy's fork clinked against her plate. "What did you say?"

Walt's booming laugh echoed in the kitchen. "I'm afraid I turned her down, which leaves us with a job."

My aunt blinked and stared at Walt. "What type of job? I'm not running for mayor either."

He squeezed her hand. "I didn't mean for you to. We have to canvas the town, without drawing attention of course, and see if a new candidate rises from the pool of Seldom Seen." He pushed his silver-rimmed glasses up on his nose. "I'm sure there is someone who would want to make a mark on the town. Perhaps one of the town council members or business owners."

"I would love to see a woman run." She glanced at me.

I raised my hand in front of my face. "No thank you. I'm not into politics, and you have to play the game to fit the role. My opinions would fly out of my mouth, and I'd be fired."

Aunt Cordy held my hand. "Let's pray about it and hope for the best."

Sounded good to me. In the meantime, who murdered the former mayor? The puzzle beaconed me to use my wits and good sense to solve it.

#####

Tuesday morning, after a day of playing catch-up on the homestead, I drove into town. A breeze blew through my car as I sailed along with the windows down. A kaleidoscope of autumn leaves fluttered to the ground from the treelined road. An earthy, sweet smell rose from the ditches. October in the mountains equaled calm for me, except for the mystery hanging in the air.

In front of Read Past Bedtime, I parallel parked. Shades of gold, scarlet, and tangerine wrapped the window displays, while books with purple and blue covers shined for patrons to see. Janine had created an attractive display to draw in folks as the tourist season wound down. In November and December, she had told me she counted on holiday sales.

I pushed the door open, and a jingle alerted her to my presence. She rose from behind the counter and shoved her long red hair behind her. Her pale but glowing skin and bright eyes reminded me of a picture book character. I had trouble believing she had turned thirty-five a few weeks ago. Youthfulness exuded from her. Aunt Cordy had shared that Janine dated a fellow in Taylors, and she thought they'd marry. I wished her the best.

"Good morning." She reached out with her arms to hug me. I'm not a big hugger, but I appreciate one from a friend.

"I love the window display. All the color drew me in. I also spied a book I might want to read." I placed both hands on the counter. "Did you recover from the festival? We have one more day to go. I'm glad Aunt Cordy planned the final weekend for only one day."

"Me too. Loading books is a heavy job, but I've had a blast. Reading to the children is a joy." She blew a wisp of hair out of her eyes. "I've gotten behind here. All of a sudden, an influx of online orders has hit my website. Thankfully, all the books are here. I was afraid I might have sold some of them at the festival. I've got to box them and address them, update the catalog and..." She stopped and took a breath. "You aren't looking for a part-time job, are you? I know you help your aunt and take photographs for Laurel's blog, but I need trusted help." She exhaled.

The offer to work in a bookstore sent a thrill through me. Any time I could hang out with books left me a happy camper, or should I say reader. In all of my travels, books kept me grounded. I had come across some fascinating bookshops and libraries, even one on the back of a donkey. The librarian had carried books covered in dust from the dirt streets, but the content fascinated me as I learned about the history and culture of the areas I visited. Plus, as much as I loved working on the homestead, I needed more to keep me busy. Of course, solving the mayor's murder engaged my mind, but working in the bookstore sounded like a fun and fulfilling job. Plus, part-time fit my needs.

I studied Janine's face filled with desperation. Lines creased at the corners of her eyes and red streaks ran across the whites. "Have you had any sleep in the last few days?"

She shook her head. "I pulled an all-nighter last night. Not my best decision, but I wanted to get ahead on the orders. I have my first children's story time in the store this afternoon. If you could cover the counter, I'd be most appreciative."

"Oh. You mean today?" Her tired eyes plead with me. "Okay. Let me call my aunt and tell her I won't be there this afternoon." I stepped outside and climbed into my car, then dialed the phone.

After one ring, she answered. "Hey. I'm going to help Janine for today."

"No worries. I've finished my chores for the day, and I'm going to rest."

We said our goodbyes and disconnected.

Back inside the store, I assured Janine I'd hang around.

"Great, let me go over the cash register and the catalog to help find the books. It's not much different from the electronic card catalogs at the library. You won't need to see the back end of the software unless you consider working for me on a regular basis." Her mouth curved into a small smile.

After a quick lesson, she excused herself to the back room to finish some work and for lunch. She ordered sandwiches from the Gathering Place for both of us, and Renee delivered them. Mine waited in the refrigerator in the workroom.

No one entered the store, so I browsed the shelves and familiarized myself with the various book sections. She carried a wide range of reading material for a small town. One section featured local authors. I had special regard for anyone who could write a story or any kind of book. Friends had suggested I write one about my time as a photographer in foreign countries, but I doubted I could sit still long enough to finish. Perhaps one of the local authors might help me. Someday, maybe.

I had squatted in the children's area to flip through a Kevin Henkes picture book when the bell jingled. I pushed the book into its slot and rose. The man who had upset Walter flipped through a travel magazine. Aunt Cordy had said he lived in Greenville now. What did he want? Oh yeah, a book.

"Good afternoon. Can I help you?" I hoped he wanted to browse instead of me pointing him to a book, since my knowledge of the store was limited.

He glanced from the magazine to me. “I wondered if you had a local history section. I’m new to this area, and I’d like to learn more.”

I guided him to the local history shelved near the local authors. “If I can help with anything else, give me a shout.”

My first customer served. Relief and joy flooded me. Once he settled into one of Janine’s blue comfy chairs, I perched on the stool behind the counter. Before I shook the mouse to wake up the screen, the bell jingled again. Walt walked in. Great, Walt and Jasper in the same room. “Hi, Walt.”

“Hello, Lyndie. Are you working for Janine?” He stood in front of me, his back to Jasper.

“For now. She needed some extra help today. Can I help you find something?”

He pulled a book out of his bag. “I’m searching for the sequel to this one.”

I took the book and read the back cover. A mystery about a man who disappeared for years, then returned home after he’d been involved in nefarious business. I shook the mouse and then typed in the author’s name. Book two sat on the shelf near the back of the store in the mystery and thrillers section. I led Walt around the shelving hoping to avoid Jasper. Of course, they ran right into each other. I watched Walt’s neck turn red.

“What are you doing here?” He stared at Jasper.

“Shopping for a book, like you.” A smug smile crossed his face.

"There's a large bookstore in Greenville. Why not shop there?" Walt inhaled a deep breath.

Jasper held up the book. "When I looked online, this is the store that carried this book. The other store didn't have any copies. Don't worry, I'm not going to see Cordelia. I got your message."

Both men eased their shoulders. Walt stuck out his hand to shake. "Sorry. I'm pretty protective, maybe too much."

Jasper shook his hand. "No worries. I understand. Cordelia is a treasure. Wish I'd not been so dumb when I was young."

He nodded to me, then walked to the front of the store and placed the book on the counter. After pressing a few wrong buttons, then the correct ones, I checked out his purchase.

He turned to Walt. "Got a question for you. Did you ever figure out who killed your mayor?"

"Not yet. Why?" Walt's brow wrinkled.

"I'd met him a time or two in Charleston, and no one minded when he left our fine town. He tried to run for mayor there, but of course the town is so big, no one knew who he was. He owned a business in Charleston for a few years. Not the friendliest or easiest to work with. As a matter of fact, he used a different name. He went by Happy Richards. Happy he wasn't."

Interesting. Why change his name? I piped in. "What type of business?"

Chapter Nineteen

The fragrance of fresh ink on new books mingled with the musty odor of the tomes from days gone by, while Walt and I stared at each other. The news Jasper shared surprised us both.

Janine hustled from the back room of the bookstore with the scent of garlic trailing her. "We have customers. Lovely." She clapped her hands together.

"You know Walt." I waved my hand at the other man. "This is Jasper." I paused in hopes he'd say his last name.

"Jasper Blake." He shook her hand. "Are you the owner of this wonderful shop?"

"I am. Thanks for coming by." She turned to me. "You ready for lunch?"

Before I stepped away, I tried to send Walt a mental signal to discover what business the mayor owned in Charleston. Then I excused myself for lunch.

In the tidy back room, shelves of books lined one wall. Along the opposite wall, the shelving held glue, bone folders, and book tape, among other items used to repair books, shipping supplies, as well as display stands and an array of decor. I grabbed my sandwich from the fridge and scooted a chair to the door. Walt and Jasper stood in the aisle near the backroom. If I chewed without making a sound, I could listen to Walt and Jasper's conversation.

Jasper spoke first. "Old Happy Richards considered himself a seasoned businessman. He oversaw the construction of condos in a town near Charleston. He had cut corners, and his cheating ways caught up with him. One of his contractors reported him, and he was fired. He had bragged about this big construction business he owned, then we all found out he was a construction manager fired for not following safety protocols and cheating the buyers." He paused. "I'm not privy to all the details, but he had some enemies. No wonder he moved away and changed his name."

Walt chimed in. "We had no idea. He presented ID when he ran for mayor, plus commendations for work he had done to improve areas where he had lived. He lied to us and must have created false documents."

"Yeah, he probably did. Listen, I've got to get back to Greenville."

"Thanks for the info."

I swallowed my last bite, tossed my wrapper, and hustled out to catch Walt.

"Hey. I listened to the conversation you had with Jasper." I twitched my lips.

Walt smiled. "I knew if I led him to the back of the store you might listen to the conversation."

"Thanks. Sounds like the mayor caused problems before he arrived in our little town. Of course, his past doesn't mean someone should have killed him, but gee whiz, what a jerk." I spotted the Kim Garee book I had wanted to read and pulled it from the shelf. "His information opens up the guilty list more than I'd hoped. Keep your ears open."

"It sure does. I'm heading out to see your aunt. I'll tell her what we discovered."

"See you later." I walked him to the front, then paid for the book I carried.

Janine cashed me out while I watched how she performed the transaction. "I heard their conversation. I have to say, I'm shocked by the mayor's behavior. We all saw him as an upstanding man."

"Sometimes people fool you." I tucked my book under the counter. "How much longer do you need me today?"

"Can you stay until after story time? I close early today and then go to the library for my writers' group. If you stay, I can get a few more packages ready to ship before the kiddos show up."

"You never get enough of books, do you?"

"Never." She flicked her red locks over her shoulder and sashayed to the back room.

While I waited for the next customers to stop in, I straightened books on the shelves.

At two o'clock, Janine twirled her way out of the back room wearing a princess dress and tall cone hat with gauzy fabric hanging from the peak.

"You're lovely."

She curtsied. "Thank you." A blush colored her cheeks.

At two-fifteen, children and parents clamored through the door for the afternoon story time. The kids gathered around the princess and oohed and aahed over her costume. Her lilting voice sang as she read about a child who wandered the forest in search of a unicorn.

A parent I remembered from the festival approached the counter. "My neighbor said you and your sister are trying to solve the mayor's murder." She paused, and I waited. The woman had something on her mind.

"I overheard June Bower, the day before he died, tell her niece she wanted to throttle him for firing her. Of course, June deserved to be let go after what she did." The woman barely took a breath.

I scratched my head. "I didn't know."

She leaned across the counter. "They were sitting in the cafe sipping coffee, and she didn't care who heard her. She also mentioned how much Otis Reardon hated the mayor, and she couldn't tolerate Otis. Yet, she works for him. Crazy, right?"

I nodded and hoped story time ended soon. "Sounds interesting. Thanks." I ducked under the counter and prayed she'd walk away. When I raised up, she had meandered to the children's area, and one of the fathers approached.

"Are you Lyndie?"

"I am."

"I've seen you at church but never met you. Your aunt has been so generous to us. She visited our homeschooling co-op and taught the children about raising apples and making products from them." He handed me a card with the co-op's name and website, plus his hand-written phone number. "Would you be interested in giving a talk about your travels and your job as a photojournalist? I think the kids would love it." His green eyes sparkled in the sunlight, and he wore no ring. Guilt poked at me for even looking.

"I'd love to. Thanks for the invite." I tucked the card into my pocket.

"Wonderful. Give me a call. I can set you up with the older students' unit."

At the end of the story time, several parents purchased books, including the handsome dad. Ring or no ring, no doubt his wife waited for him at home.

Janine had changed into her street clothes and joined me at the desk. "I see you met Mr. Single Dad. He's a cutie, isn't he?"

"Um...sure. He seemed nice." Nope, I wasn't going there. First Zach, now him. I didn't need distractions.

Janine may have sensed my lack of enthusiasm and changed the subject. "Thanks for helping out today. I'd love to have you work one or two days a week. What do you think?"

"Let me talk to Aunt Cordy. I promised to help her as much as possible." Although I'd love to work in the bookstore and have more financial independence. "I'll call you."

Outside, the sun shimmered through the tree limbs and reminded me even on cooler days, the sun still warmed the earth. Before I drove home, I slipped down the street to Toolsmith Hardware. They closed at five, so I had an hour to snoop.

I crept inside the store. No one manned the front counter, so I shuffled along the wall and entered a center aisle. Otis's voice bellowed from somewhere in the back of the hardware. "June, where'd you put the new hoses I ordered? UPS delivered them yesterday."

June's voice sounded from the back. "I told you I couldn't lift them to put them on the shelf you wanted them on. Why don't you listen to me?"

He raised his voice more. "I hired you to work, woman. Not whine."

I pressed myself against the shelf as June hurried past me. "I quit." The front door slammed. Not sure I wanted to be alone in the store with Otis, I tiptoed toward the door.

"Lyndie Lavender, can I help you?" Otis's eyes shot daggers at me. Goosebumps popped on my arms.

I turned to face him. "Sure. Aunt Cordy wanted me to pick up some more of your small baskets for apples." Quick thinking was never my strength.

"Interesting. She picked up several last week." A tight smile flattened his lips. "As a matter of fact, she took all I had."

Why hadn't I paid attention to what my aunt carried home? "Then I'd better go."

"Not so fast. Did you see June leave?" His eyes narrowed.

"I did. She about knocked me down." I choked out a strained giggle.

He rubbed his chin with his chubby hand. "She'll be back. She needs this job."

Don't be so sure. I scuttled out of the store and hurried across the street. June sat in the gazebo in the town square, her head in her hands. I climbed the steps and lowered myself onto the bench.

"June." She raised her head and stared at me.

"You heard him, didn't you? You listened to him yell at me." Her eyes pleaded with me to agree. "I saw you as I ran out."

I patted her arm. "Yes, I did."

"I'm not going back. I'll starve first." A tear trickled down her face.

"No one is going to let you starve. Have you searched for another job?" If she had killed the mayor, she'd have free meals in jail. Oops. I shouldn't go there.

She wrung her hands until an angry red colored them. "I found out yesterday I can claim my social security. With a monthly check and a part-time job, I'll have enough."

Poor June's life had not gone well. "I'm glad you have a plan. You've earned every penny and deserve to get it." The conversation between Walt and Jasper rolled in my mind. Did I come out and ask her or ignore my concerns? "June, can I ask you something?"

"I guess." A worry line creased her forehead.

"I overheard something. Someone said you had wanted to throttle the mayor. Is that true?" I waited. She stilled beside me and glared at me like she wanted to throttle me.

Then, she twisted her lips and stared at the ground. A sigh blew from her mouth, and she lifted her face to me. "The only person I've confided in about my hatred of the mayor is my niece, and she'd never share. What a horrendous accusation?"

"Doesn't matter, but if you killed the mayor, you need to confess." I stood to leave.

June rose beside me. "You were my friend. How can you believe I murdered the mayor? I may have been angry with him, but I didn't kill him. I left the festival with my niece. Ask the police. I told them where I was." She gritted her teeth and snarled. "Leave me alone." She darted from the gazebo and left me standing.

Most people spoke out of turn and said things they didn't mean. I've done it myself. June spouted to her niece in public. Not cool. With June's short stature, I doubted she could've swung the apple butter paddle hard enough to knock him down. I'd take her off the list for sure.

My heart hurt for the woman. She'd married young, her husband had died, and she reestablished herself in Seldom Seen and lived a decent life until she ruined the mural. One mistake didn't mean she couldn't start over. I'd keep my ears open for a possible part-time job she'd like.

Before any more trouble found me, I trekked to my car. On the way, Jasper caught my eye. He walked along the sidewalk with Johnson Winters and Marcy Fox. Friends? Acquaintances? Accomplices? Or getting to know the townspeople? This day got curiouser and curiouser.

Chapter Twenty

When the Wednesday morning drizzle ended, I marveled at how the cloudy, gray sky enhanced the rich hues of the green grass and the red and gold leaves on the maple trees. Water droplets coated the sheep's meadow as they pranced to meet me at the fence.

"Good morning, ladies." Their off-white curls bounced as they skipped to me. I entered the pen and filled their feed and water. They followed me across the grass. Inside their shed, I knocked down some cobwebs, then plopped on the bench. The smell of hay filled the little building. Good thing I wasn't allergic.

Thimble nuzzled my leg. "Hey, beautiful." I ran my hand through her luxurious fleece. Floss nudged me with her head. "You're a beauty too. I won't leave you out." With my hands on both animals, I longed to go back to enjoying the simple life, but I was determined to catch the person who had killed the mayor. I worked hard on Aunt Cordy's farm, but the lack of stress compared to my former life brought me joy, even if at times a bit of boredom crept in.

"What do you think?" I spoke out loud to my sheep. "Who do you think knocked the mayor in the head?"

Both sheep baaed at me. I studied their dark faces, their eyes the same color as their faces. Who stepped into the dark place and clobbered the man in charge of the town? Who hated him enough to cause him harm? I had read people killed over greed, love, power, and revenge. Which one fit this situation? Who fit the crime? The word *love* screamed in my head. Oh, my goodness. I hadn't considered...

Floss butted my leg with her head again, and my whole body startled. "What's up, girly?" I held her face in my hands. Jesus protected his sheep and searched for the lost one. Whoever caused the mayor's death must feel lost, or had the person become so calloused they didn't care? No matter what, I had to ferret out the guilty one. Sure, I had confidence in Danny and the police department, but for Aunt Cordy's sake and mine, I'd keep searching for clues.

I tugged my phone from my pocket and dialed Laurel.

"Hey." She sounded hurried.

"What are you doing this afternoon?" I twirled a piece of hay in my fingers.

"I'm taking Danny his lunch. He's had a tough week, so I made him the chicken salad he likes. Afterward, I planned to drop in on some of the town businesses and see if they needed anything added to their page on the blog. I check in from time to time."

"Perfect. I'll tag along." I pushed fluff out of Floss's eyes. "I can bring my camera and snap some photos to refresh the pages."

She sighed. "What are you up to?"

"I have a new hunch about the mayor's murder. I'm hoping to gather clues."

"Be here at my house by eleven, so I can deliver Danny's lunch at eleven thirty."

"Thanks, Sis." I clicked off the call then petted the sheep one last time, before I jogged to the house.

"You in a hurry?" Aunt Cordy stepped away from me in the hallway.

"I'm sorry." I placed a hand on her shoulder. "I'm meeting Laurel in town in an hour. Do you need me to do anything or pick up anything?"

"Can you stop at the store and buy two bags of sugar? The apple butter took all I had." She stared into my face. "Did you hear me?"

"Of course. Two bags of sugar." Aunt Cordy's eyebrows raised, and I almost heard her wheels turn. The frown on her face told me I might as well fess up.

"Laurel is visiting several of the businesses this afternoon, and I'm tagging along to take pictures, and do a little eavesdropping and clue gathering."

She patted my arm. "Good girl. If the police don't find the killer, I trust you will." She watched my face. "Don't look so surprised. I want the person caught as much as you do. It happened on my property."

"You're the reason I want to find them." We hugged our aunt-niece-hug, one filled with warmth and love. I'd do anything for this woman.

At eleven o'clock, I parked in front of Laurel's home. Oak and maple trees stood like towers in the front yard. A tire swing hung from a low branch. An aqua-blue door welcomed visitors to the cottage-style home, and pots of lavender chrysanthemums graced the entry.

Laurel had decorated our room when we were young. She'd hung swaths of pink organza over our windows and talked Mom into buying pink and purple handwoven rugs for the floor. Two things we could move with us when we traveled to a new mission home. Hard to admit, but they brought comfort and eased the trial of moving. Ironic how I disliked moving as a child but spent my adult life roaming the continents. Thank goodness I landed at my aunt's, where I planned to stay.

Laurel opened the front door. "Come in." I entered and followed her to the kitchen.

"Want a sandwich?" She handed me chicken salad on wheat bread. My taste buds savored a bite. "Delicious. You make the best. Close to mom's, but yours has a unique flavor." I took another bite.

"I add a hint of dill to mine." Laurel ate her sandwich as she packed Danny's. I admired my sister, the juggler of all things family, church, and community.

Half an hour later, we stepped into Danny's office and delivered his lunch.

"Hey, ladies." His gaze bounced between us. "Both sisters today, huh. How are you, Lyndie? Have you dug up any more clues?" He chuckled. I didn't divulge my intentions for the afternoon.

"If you share, I will too."

He bit into his sandwich. After he swallowed, he put his sandwich on the desk and lifted a folder. "Everything we've gathered points to someone the mayor knew and trusted. We have a few suspects, and we're narrowing it down. Please stay out of the way and don't get yourself in trouble." His eyebrows furrowed, and the corners of his mouth turned down. Uh oh, his serious face.

No actual information from Danny today. Oh well, on to spying, or should I say visiting businesses.

The fresh scent of lavender and an earthy fragrance met our noses when we opened the door to the Baa Baa Black Sheep shop. Jonquil posed at her loom while I snapped photos, and Laurel jotted notes for an upcoming sale.

While Laurel and Jonquil chatted, I photographed several of the handwoven pieces she had scattered throughout the shop. The softness of the scarves translated well to my camera. The women in Guatemala had woven wraps for Laurel and me.

When I finished taking pictures, I joined the ladies at the counter. A rainbow of hand-dyed hanks of yarn hung from pegs behind the counter. I'd come back for some of the cotton yarn to use in my embroidery projects. As soon as I found the time to create handwork again.

Jonquil leaned toward Laurel. "I think someone who was jealous of the mayor did him in. Someone who either wanted his mayoral position, or someone who fell for him and he paid them no mind. Just my opinion, of course."

Interesting. I had similar ideas about jealousy and greed being two powerful enemies of kindness and love.

Laurel chimed in. "I don't disagree with you, but who around here found the mayor to be a catch?"

Good question. We said goodbye to Jonquil and stopped by Astrid Perry's shop, Whimsical Charm. She hosted local artists and artisans in her shop. Seldom Seen embraced our local artists and creators. Blessed to visit this incredible store of eclectic styles and offerings, I hoped someday to add my fiber work. Of course, I had to make something first.

Astrid waved us to her desk in the center of the store. She stood. "I'm so glad you stopped in." She nodded her head toward the corner, and we followed. In a whisper, she shared some shocking news. "Someone told me you two are trying to solve the mayor's murder. I hate to even say the word, but I wanted to tell you something." Her eyes rounded, and her eyebrows raised. "Did you know the mayor had been married before he came to Seldom Seen? He left his family and relocated. Then he told all of us he'd been a bachelor his whole life. He even asked me out on a date. I turned him down. He wasn't my type." She fluffed her hair. "I thought you'd want to know."

"Where did you hear that?" Laurel rubbed the back of her neck, my sister's telltale sign she was ruminating on the information. When her kids asked her about going somewhere or doing something, she rubbed her neck.

"Marcy Fox told me. She has a legit source for her information, or so she says. I'm not sure I trust her, but I think she may be telling the truth this time." Astrid straightened a watercolor on the wall behind us.

"Thanks." I considered this as a clue, not to the murder, but at least to the mayor's life. If he had to start over, he had come to a wonderful town. No, perhaps not for him, considering what happened.

After we left Whimsical Charm, Laurel and I rested on one of the benches scattered around town. "Astrid's intel stunned me. I had no idea our illustrious leader had a secret life."

"He sure did. Married, and with a business and a different name in Charleston."

"What?" Laurel stared at me with her big-sister stare.

"I forgot to tell you. Jasper, Aunt Cordy's old beau, told Walt Mayor Richardson went by Happy Richards and ran a construction company. He had told people he owned the company, but he didn't. They fired him."

"The plot grows deeper. I believe our mayor was a conniver. No wonder he sweet-talked the town council and got his way about most everything. Granted, he improved the town, but, geesh, what a cad." She pounded her fist on her leg.

"Did you say cad?" I grinned at my sister, who made it her ambition to learn a new word every day.

"I did. The term is fitting." She rose from the bench. "Let's make one more stop. Leo wanted me to update his page. He has some new items to sell."

I hoped Leo allowed me into his store after our encounter at the river.

Inside Leo Randolph's Whittlers Woodworking, the fragrance of fresh-cut wood soothed me. Our grandfather had built furniture, and I had a distant memory of playing in his wood shop. He had cut blocks for us grandkids to stack and build with. Anytime I smelled cut wood, he came to mind.

Leo sat at his worktable carving a bird on a branch. "Laurel and Lyndie, did you come to see my latest work?" He notched out a groove to add a feather.

"We did. Lyndie can take photos of your recent additions, and I'll jot some notes." She lifted a notebook from her large leather bag.

He rested his tool on the table and blew some shavings from his latest creation. "Follow me."

A row of gorgeous birds rested on a display shelf near the front of the store. A tiny hummingbird tucked its beak into a hollyhock bloom. I gasped at how real the bluebird perched on a birdhouse looked. The goldfinch resting on the thistle was going home with me. "Leo, these are amazing. They're so realistic." I snapped photos while he told Laurel the name of each sculpture.

"I'm working on an indigo bunting to add to the collection." Pride colored his face as he grinned at his work.

"I'd love to buy the goldfinch. They're one of my favorite birds." I studied the beautiful yellow and black bird and the purple thistle it sat on.

Leo shuffled his feet. "The goldfinch isn't for sale. As a matter of fact, none of these are for sale."

Laurel watched the man fidget. "Why add them to your Something Seen page, then?"

"Let's not. I made them for a friend who loves birds, but they don't want them. I'd sell them, but I can't." He glanced around the store. "Lyndie, is there something else you'd like?" His voice shook as he spoke.

I placed a hand on his arm. "How about I come back another time when I can browse?"

"Sure." He shuffled to his workbench and sat. Sorrow etched his face.

Chapter Twenty-One

Laurel stepped into the bright sunlight, a contrast from the gray clouds earlier today. Several folks hustled on the sidewalks. The fragrance of homemade bread wafted from Baker's Delight. I waved at Janine across the street at Read Past Bedtime.

Laurel squinted and took my hand. "We need sugar." She tugged me into the bakery. Delight straightened the few items left on her shelves. By two fifty in the afternoon, we had less than ten minutes to satisfy our desire for baked goods.

"Hi, ladies. What can I get you? Everything is half price at the end of the day."

Laurel took charge, as usual. "Sounds good. We'll take the last two scones."

"They're cranberry walnut, my personal favorite." She used tongs to place them into a small white bag. "Would you like coffee or tea?"

"Lady Grey, please. In a to-go cup." I adjusted the strap on my camera.

Laurel held out cash. "Me too."

Our favorite baker offered us cups with sleeves. Steam rose from the sipping holes in the lids, and a light spicy fragrance filled the air.

"Thanks, Delight." My sister took the bag of scones and hurried me out the door to the town's gazebo. Painted white with a scrolled gingerbread trim, the structure welcomed townspeople and visitors.

We ate and enjoyed the quiet until she couldn't. "That was weird."

"Delight or Leo?" I sipped my tea.

Laurel stared at me. "Leo, of course. Who do you think he made the birds for?"

"I have a hunch they're for June. Our wonderful, I mean annoying, town grapevine spread a rumor that he has a thing for her." The last bite of cranberry and walnut left my taste buds happy. Delight's skills in the kitchen exceeded the best bakery chefs. "He wanted to impress her with his skills, and she rejected him." Yep, unrequited love.

Laurel wadded the bag and tossed it into the trash can. "Isn't he too old for her?"

"I'm not sure. She's ready to collect Social Security, so she's in her sixties. I'd place him somewhere in his seventies. How strong do you think he is?"

Understanding dawned on my sister. "Do you think he hit the mayor?"

"It's a theory, but I'm not sure. He's laid back most of the time, but he and June screamed at each other at the river." I tapped my finger on my mouth. "He grew up here, and people love him and his carvings. He used to compete and win ribbons for his work." I tossed my cup away. "Plus, he and his nephew designed a vector program to generate carving patterns. They say he made serious money when he sold it." I brushed crumbs off my pants. "Of course, that's hearsay."

"We should find out more about him. Walt might have more info." She rubbed her hands together and then peeked at her phone. "Want to go with me to pick up the kids?"

We stood. "No. I'm going to walk to your house and get my car. It's a beautiful day, and I may make a stop along the way."

Laurel hugged me, and I stepped out of the gazebo on a mission.

Purple asters and yellow pansies lined the walk to Walt's house. I tapped on his front door, a traditional white on his yellow-sided home, then waited a few minutes, but no one answered. Disappointment tugged at me until I saw Leo. I hid behind a bush in front of Walt's home. What was Leo doing? He sat on the porch of a small sky-blue bungalow with white trim, two houses down from Walt. A compact car pulled into the driveway. I tiptoed across the front of the house next door to get a better spot to spy. Yes, spy. Might as well admit what I did. June Bower and her niece, Luna, climbed out of the car. I lifted my camera and snapped photos of them.

Leo stood and then sashayed to the end of the sidewalk.

"What are you doing here?" June fisted her hands and let them hang at her sides. "I told you not to come to Luna's house."

"Juney, I want to give you the birds. The ones I made for you. Somebody came to the shop today and wanted to buy one of them, but I worked on them for months as a gift for you." He held his hands in front of him as if he begged her to take them.

She swiped her hand through the air. "I told you no. I don't want the birds. I have nowhere to put them since I moved in with my niece. Sell them to whoever wants them. And don't call me Juney." She turned away from him, pulled a tote bag from the car, and then slammed the door. She faced him on the sidewalk. "You need to leave now." She marched to the house, and Luna followed.

I shimmied along the house I hid beside until I reached Walt's place, where I smacked into a cedar bush.

"Lyndie?"

I slapped my hand over my face to muffle a scream. My heart triple thumped, and my legs shook. "Walt. You scared me."

He bit his lip. I'm guessing he wanted to laugh but didn't want to hurt my feelings. "It's okay. You can laugh at me. I was watching an interaction between Leo and June. He's got it bad for her, but she's not interested. Do you think he was jealous of the mayor?"

Walt shifted a brown paper bag to his other arm and unlocked his front door. "Come in, and we'll talk." He held the door open for me. Inside, a living room spread out on one side, with brown upholstered furniture. A dining area with an old oak table and chairs sat on the opposite side. The white walls held a few paintings and portraits of family. His furniture stood practical and sturdy, like Walt.

"Have a seat on the couch while I put my groceries away." After a few minutes, he joined me.

He lowered himself into a leather recliner opposite me. "What were you doing outside?"

I folded my hands in my lap. "I stopped to talk to you, but you weren't home. When I went to leave, I saw Leo a couple of houses over, so I'm embarrassed to say, I slid over to the next house and eavesdropped and took pictures. Not my best moment, but we've got to figure out who killed the mayor. I don't like the fact it happened on Aunt Cordy's property."

He nodded several times. "Has Danny gotten any closer to solving the case?"

"He won't tell me much except to mind my business. I want to tell him, I *am* minding my business, protecting my aunt." I sank into the couch.

"Let's see the photos." He moved to sit beside me on the couch.

I opened the photos, and we flipped through them together. Walt pointed at Leo's face. "The sorrow on his face breaks my heart. The puppy dog frown he's giving June shows a man filled with sorrow."

"June refuses to accept his gift of carved birds he made her. They're beautiful too. Laurel and I stopped by his shop, and I asked if I could buy one, but he said no." I moved through the photos to the ones I took in Leo's shop. "Look at these. They're remarkable."

"Those are incredible. The detail makes them appear real."

I scanned back to the photos I'd snapped in front of Luna's house. "She's telling him to leave in this one."

Walt leaned closer. "Who is in the background?"

I enlarged the shot. "Johnson Winters. His truck is in the driveway across the street. I was so focused on Leo and June, I didn't notice him, but he sure is ogling them. June raised her voice, and poor Luna stood and watched."

"Johnson may have been doing a job over there and heard their voices." Walt studied the photo and then glanced at me. "You said you'd come to talk to me. What did you want?"

I clicked the camera button off and laid it beside me. "Laurel and I wondered if you knew much about Leo."

Walt rubbed his nose beneath his glasses. "We attended school together. He's a few years older than I am, and he graduated as salutatorian. He quarterbacked the high school football team and took classes at the community college. As I recall, he stayed nearby to help his mom. She passed about five years after graduation, and Leo stayed in the house he grew up in. Never married or had kids. He spent his life creating wood carvings and furniture. His knack for math shows in his creations."

"Did he and a nephew make a computer program?"

"They did. He was proud of his nephew. Sad thing is the boy passed away a few years ago." He rubbed his chin. "Far as I know,

Leo has never even had a parking ticket. He's about as good as possible. Minds his own business and goes to church."

The information Walt fed me tumbled in my brain. "Maybe he's not the person to watch, then. Sounds like he's lovesick, is all."

Walt patted my arm. "Lyndie, please be careful nosing around. I'll do whatever I can to help. I love your aunt and don't want this hanging over her head either, but I don't want you to get hurt."

Walt's sincere confession of love for my aunt gave me goosebumps. I loved her too, and I wanted the best for her. "I promise to be cautious and pay attention. I'm not convinced Otis didn't hit the mayor with the apple butter stirrer. He's got a mean streak. He yelled at June the other day at the store. It was abusive, if you asked me."

"He's been a miserable human most of his life. His dad was rough on him as a kid, but that's no excuse for his behavior as an adult. I believe we all have choices to make when we grow up. I choose to be a better person."

I stood to leave. "You are an amazing person, Walt. I'm so happy Aunt Cordy has you in her life. By the way, you haven't changed your mind about running for mayor, have you? You have plenty of time to prepare."

He chuckled. "You are relentless, aren't you?"

"But, you didn't say no."

He opened the front door. "Thanks for dropping by."

"Thank you for listening to me." I waved and walked down the sidewalk toward Laurel's house.

In front of Luna's house, a package on the porch stopped me. Of course, a cardboard box was none of my business, but since I had been spying, I sneaked to the cement slab on the front of the house and peeked at the package. I snapped a quick photo, then darted away. Around the corner, I opened my camera's photos. The address label had Luna's name. The return was from an art store in Ashville. Nothing to see here.

I hurried to Laurel's house and found an envelope tucked under my windshield wiper. What now? After I packed my camera into the case and tucked it behind the driver's seat, I lifted the wiper, retrieved the envelope and climbed into my car. Before I opened the seal, someone knocked on my window, and I jumped. I turned, and Laurel's eyes met mine. I cranked the window down with the old-fashioned roller. "You made me jump."

"Sorry. I didn't know you'd still be here. What have you been doing while I picked up the kids?" She leaned against the frame of my window.

My sister, nosier than I am, had to know. "I stopped and talked to Walt." I filled her in on the conversation and the altercation between June and Leo. She narrowed her eyes as I ended my story.

"What's in the envelope?"

I held it in front of my face and flipped it around. "I was deciding whether to open it now or at home."

She snatched it from me. "Now is good."

Chapter Twenty-Two

I slid out of my Jeep and stood beside Laurel. Birds chirped on the quiet maple and oak-lined street, and a brown bunny hopped across the yard. Henry and Josephine tossed their book bags onto the porch, then Josephine practiced cartwheels, and Henry climbed his favorite tree.

If only my heart calmed with the rhythm of the peaceful scene. I plucked the envelope from Laurel's hand. "I'll open it. Let's sit on the porch."

Laurel and I settled onto her white porch swing. I stared at the paper envelope in my hand and prayed whatever it said inside gave us another clue. With nothing written on the outside, I had no idea who had left it.

My sister pumped her legs and moved the swing back and forth. "Are you going to stare at it or open it?"

I ran my finger under the glued flap and loosened it enough to lift it. A piece of yellow legal paper peeked out. I withdrew the sheet of paper and unfolded it. Written in red crayon, the words BACK OFF jumped at me.

"Whoa, someone is sending you a warning. Funny, it's written in crayon." Laurel stopped the swing. She held her hand out for the paper. I handed it to her. She lifted it to the sunlight. "Hmm...something was written on the page on top of this one." She held it in front of me. Sure enough, an indentation appeared.

She hopped off the swing. "Come in the house with me."

I tagged along behind my sister like a golden retriever followed its owner. She rummaged in a drawer in the kitchen for a pencil and directed me to sit at the table. Yes, she did both things at the same time. She joined me, then laid the yellow sheet of paper on the table. With the pencil and a light hand, she scribbled over the page. Sure enough, numbers appeared.

"Someone has been doing math on the previous page or at least on top of this one. I can't make out what they were working on, but there are faint scribbles of addition and subtraction with a few marks I can't identify." Laurel handed it to me. "What do you think?"

"The markings might be inches or quotation marks. I'm not sure. They could be random too. Whoever wrote the numbers must have been working on a project of some sort, or their kid's homework. Otis might have been adding or subtracting something at the store. I'll stop in and see if he uses lined yellow paper." I smoothed the page in front of me. Why red crayon? Red means stop, or he wanted to get my attention. "I wonder how whoever left this knew to find my Jeep at your house. Do you think they followed me?"

Laurel touched my arm. "First, I don't want you going to the hardware store by yourself. If it was Otis, he might get out of line and threaten you. Second, the red crayon makes the words leap off the page. I use red on the website to draw attention. Would he put that much thought into it?"

I placed my hand on Laurel's. "I'm heading home. When I see Zach, I'll talk to him and ask what he's doing tomorrow. If he's available, I'll ask him to go with me."

"Sounds good. I don't want you to get hurt or even yelled at. I've been on the other end of Otis's anger. One time I flubbed his ad on the blog, and he pitched a fit. I fixed it as soon as I could, but he glared at me every time I saw him for a week." She walked me to the steps.

I hugged her. "Thanks for your help. I have to pick up sugar for Aunt Cordy, then I want see my sheep." I waved at my niece and nephew. "Goodbye, you two."

When I pulled the Jeep into the driveway, I parked it beside the barn. Floss and Thimble hopped to the fence. "Hey, cuties." I left my bag in the Jeep and trotted to the gate. Inside, I cuddled my sheep. "You ladies smell stinky, but I love you." I ran my hands over their fluff and into the thick undercoat. The lanolin left my hands softer. "I've had a day." Inside their little barn, I cleaned out the dirty straw from the floor and freshened the supply. Then I filled their feed and water. Bashful and Happy's areas came next. Once I finished caring for my favorite creatures, I wiped off the bench and sat. The sheep rested their heads on each of my legs. "You two are cuddlebugs."

Footsteps sounded in the field next to the little shed. From the doorway, Zack peered in. "Hey, Lyndie."

"Hi. Come on in." He sat on the other end of the bench. "I was hoping to see you today."

He petted Floss, who left me and snuggled his knee. "Glad I stopped over. I saw your Jeep and realized I hadn't spoken to you for a few days. I've been busy with classes. We have lots of field trips to the park this time of year, so I've been teaching about the great outdoors. I'm surprised I have a voice left." He grinned his charming grin.

I imagined a lot of little girls had a crush on their nature instructor. Maybe a few single teachers, too. "Do you teach tomorrow?"

"I'm off tomorrow, since I teach Friday and Sunday afternoon. We have a tour group on Sunday who requested a tour of one of the trails. At least I'll get to attend the last day of your aunt's Apple Festival. Does she always stretch it out over three weekends?" He picked a piece of straw and twirled it in his fingers.

I rested my hand on Thimble's back. "She tried three this year but wants to go back to two next year. She said she had to work too hard to keep up with the homestead and all the prep work for the festival to do three weekends again. I'm glad she didn't add Sunday to this one. About tomorrow, I need a small favor."

He picked more straw from the floor and wove them together into a star. Impressive. "What sort of favor?"

I pulled the yellow paper from where I had tucked it in my pocket. "I found this in an envelope on my car today. Laurel and I noticed it had some math problems written on it that appeared to be measurements. I want to stop at ToolSmith Hardware tomorrow and check if Otis uses yellow legal paper in the store."

"Red crayon. Classy." He held the paper in front of him. "Did you notice this corner has initials printed? You didn't run the pencil over this spot." He pulled a pencil from his shirt pocket and scribbled. "REV. I wonder what those mean."

"The letters could refer to any number of things." He handed the page to me, and I folded it and shoved it in my pocket. "Anyway, can you go, or do you have something else you need to do? It's okay either way. Laurel made me promise not to go alone. She's afraid he'll let his temper flare and attack me. Frankly, I'm not afraid of him. His bark is bad, but his bite may not be."

*****

Thursday morning, after I stripped the beds and started the washer, I climbed into Zach's truck as he took the driver's side. We had eaten Aunt Cordy's fried apple pancakes for breakfast, topped with real maple syrup. While we enjoyed the cinnamon-flavored treat, we discussed what happened yesterday, and I revealed the note to her. She thanked Zach for joining me in my nosing around.

The blue sky promised a dry, comfortable day as Zach sailed along the road to town. In my imagination, a scenario played out where Otis would confess to hitting the mayor with Aunt Cordy's apple butter paddle and causing his demise. By the time Zach parked his truck, doubt colored my thoughts with a red crayon.

"Do you have a plan for how to discover if this is Otis's paper?" Zach held the offending piece of yellow paper.

"I didn't realize you'd picked it up. Thanks." I snatched it from his hand. "I'll find something to buy and then look at the counter while he rings up the purchase. Do you have any ideas?"

"I need a few things for a presentation tomorrow. Why don't I ask him where they are and then you can do your snoop thing." His white teeth flashed a smile.

I couldn't stop the grin from spreading across my face. "I like the way you think." Before I unbuckled my seatbelt, Zach had jogged around the truck and opened my door.

"Let's scope the place out." He teased. "Isn't that how they say it on television?"

I shook my head and strode into the hardware store, with Zach on my heels. The switch from bright sunlight to the dim interior stopped me. Zach tapped my shoulder. "You might want to take off your sunglasses."

"Guess I should." My cheeks heated. I pulled my regular glasses from the case in my purse and swapped them for my sunglasses. "I'm not sure why, but I'm nervous." Zach stood shoulder to shoulder with me. "Thanks for coming."

"No worries. We'll get this done." He ambled along the aisle, and I followed. Otis helped a customer at the counter. I didn't expect to run into June, since she had quit, and she meant never to return. No other customers browsed the shelves or bins. A faint motor oil odor reminded me of my grandpa. The old wooden floors, bowed in places from the number of steps taken on them, squeaked under my feet.

Otis must have heard us. He peered across the store and scowled. Great. He cashed out the fellow at the counter, who left, then Otis stared at me. Bless Zach, he trekked to the counter and described the items he needed while I wandered along the aisle closest to the counter. Somehow, Zach turned Otis's attention away from where I stood. Without hesitation, I scooted to the counter. Sure enough, I spied a yellow legal pad with pages torn off, a box of envelopes—and I couldn't believe my eyes—a broken red crayon. Ugh.

I pulled my phone from my pocket and snapped a few photos. Footsteps moved in my direction, so I darted into a different row of goods and pretended to find interest in a bin of penny nails. I listened as Zach and Otis conversed about Zach's use of rope and candles for his presentation. After he paid, Zach took me by the elbow, and we left the store.

Outside, I released a breath I didn't know I was holding. Why did my nerves jump like frogs today? I had photographed war zones and watched destruction for twenty years without a blink. Perhaps, finding the killer of someone I knew on a more personal level shook me more. Except for Elias and a smattering of women, I wasn't acquainted with the people in the war zones on a personal level. The ladies I had friended, who had survived, found a way to relocate. Unlike my previous encounters, the mayor's death hit us all hard, especially Aunt Cordy.

In the truck, Zach started the engine. "Did you find anything?"

I buckled my seatbelt. "Want to get a coffee at Misty Mornings Cafe? I'd like to get away from here."

"You've got it." He started the truck then pulled into the street. Within minutes, he parked in front of the little cafe with the red and white striped awning.

Inside, I ordered a lavender honey decaf latte, and Zach asked for a flat white espresso with steamed milk. When I breathed in the fragrance of ground coffee beans, my shoulders relaxed, and my heart calmed. We snagged a table in the corner, and I sipped the delicate lavender honey mix. After a few minutes of delighting in my latte, I laid my phone on the table and called up the photos I'd taken. Zach leaned in and flipped through them. "Huh. Seems suspicious to me."

"Right?" I tapped my finger on the photo of the crayon. When I did, the picture enlarged. I stared at the photo. "Do you see what's in the corner?"

Chapter Twenty-Three

Soft jazz music played in the background at the cafe. Spoons clicked against ceramic mugs, and conversations buzzed. I loved Misty Mornings' policy of using real tableware for the folks who dined inside, and the fresh flowers on every table added a personal touch and a sweet fragrance. I bet they purchased them from Rachel's flower shop.

Zach lifted my phone to take a closer look at the photo of the yellow legal paper, then placed it on the table between us. "The word is cut off in the photo, but it starts with REVEN. Could it be the beginning of REVENGE?"

"Do you think he's trying to throw us off? He may have started with the mayor, then made his list. What kind of revenge do you think he's planning?" I stared at the list again. He had written REVEN at the top, then listed names. No details or plans, simply names. My aunt, Jonquil, Marcy Fox, and another name I couldn't read. What had those women done to him? I stood from my chair. "I'm going to ask him. He can't take aim at these women and get away with it."

Zach rose to face me. "How about we show Danny?"

I chewed my lower lip. "If we show Danny, he'll know we were spying." The joy I'd found in my latte dissipated. My shoulders tensed, and my tummy rolled.

Zach pushed our chairs in. "Does it matter when someone is in danger?" For the second time today, he touched my elbow and guided me out the door. He opened the truck door, and I climbed in and sank into the seat. He settled into the driver's seat. Before I protested, he aimed the vehicle toward the police station.

Inside the station, I spotted Danny. He waved and walked toward us. "What are you two doing today?" He glanced from me to Zach with a grin on his face.

In his office, he replaced the grin with a scowl as he studied the note I'd received and the photos I'd taken. He listened as I explained where I had found the note and how Laurel and I had figured out the imprint, then how Zach and I had discovered the clues from Otis's store. His gaze rose to meet mine. "Lyndie, you should have given me the note before you and Laurel scribbled all over it, and you shouldn't have been snooping around Otis's store." He glared at Zach.

I twisted my hands in my lap. "I want to find out who killed the mayor and why Otis is seeking revenge."

He ran a hand through his blond hair. "I get it, but you have to understand I'm the one who will solve the crime. I have suspects in mind, and I'm working on it. You've got to trust the process."

Zach tapped on the desk. "It's not that we don't trust. We hoped to help. I was accused of a crime I didn't commit, so I get what it is to search for the truth."

Danny sent the photos from my phone to his and handed the device to me. "You two go home or wherever it is you can go to stay out of trouble. Help Aunt Cordy get ready for the last day of the Apple Festival, take a hike, do anything except snoop around, and please keep Laurel out of this. We have kids I'm trying to protect."

"Sorry, Danny." I hung my head as we walked out of the station.

Zach caught up with me. "A hike might be a good idea. I'm leading one tomorrow after my presentation in DuPont Forest. If we check it out today, it gives me a chance to prepare and gives you the opportunity to clear your head. What do you say?"

Zach's gentle way and kind heart, plus those dark brown eyes, were hard to say no to. "Okay. I could use the exercise."

An hour later, the truck tires crunched on the gravel in the parking lot to the trail. "I'm taking a group including some homeschool families to Hooker Falls tomorrow, then we'll hike to Triple Falls. We should finish around two o'clock. Let's head up the hill and check it out."

Thankfully, I'd worn sturdy shoes I could hike in. "I followed him along a dirt and gravel path, which wound along a mountain trail. The brilliant color of the scarlet and gold leaves against the bright blue sky made me wish I'd brought my camera. Instead, I snapped a few pictures with my phone. I tried not to let the dress down from Danny spoil God's gorgeous creation.

"Here we are." Zach and I turned a corner, and water roared over the rock wall. We stepped across several large rocks and climbed over some fallen logs to the rolling water. A cool mist kissed my face as the river flowed from the falls. A few people, scattered around the grounds, perched on rocks and soaked in the beauty of the tumbling water.

I shot a few more photos with my phone's camera. "I'd forgotten how beautiful and refreshing the falls are. This is one of the spots Laurel and I visited when we lived with Aunt Cordy, several years ago. I miss those days. We'd load our backpacks with food and take off into the woods and along the rivers." I nudged Zach with my shoulder. "Thanks."

He gave me a lopsided grin. "I hope the kids respond as well tomorrow. Some teenagers love it and some don't." He glanced at me. "You wouldn't want to come with me, would you, and give them tips about taking pictures? If you're busy, it's alright."

"Let me check with Aunt Cordy when we get home. The last day of the festival is Saturday, and I'm not sure if she needs me to help her." If she didn't, a morning in the woods sounded wonderful.

By three o'clock, Zach parked the truck in my aunt's driveway and let me out. "I'll see you at dinner. Aunt Cordy told me earlier Walt is bringing Renee's fried chicken and tater salad from The Gathering Place. She's an incredible cook. You're welcome to join us."

"Sounds good." He waved and drove to his cabin.

I hustled across the barnyard to see Floss and Thimble. They bounded through the field to me, such loyal pets. I refreshed their water and feed, gave them some pats, then searched for Aunt Cordy.

I found her in the kitchen sealing a batch of apple butter in a hot water bath. "There's my girl. I'm finished with the canning and ready to put my feet up."

Utensils and bowls filled the sink. "Let me clean up while you sit for a while."

"Thank you, sweet girl." She rested in a kitchen chair with her feet propped on a stool.

"You're welcome. What else can I do to help get ready for Saturday?" I filled the white porcelain sink with hot sudsy water, then submerged the dirty dishes. With a scouring pad, I scrubbed the bowls and spoons, then rinsed them and stacked them to dry.

Aunt Cordy took off her shoe and rubbed the side of her foot. "Tomorrow, Walt and I will double-check everything we need for Saturday. Since the weather has held, the tables and booths are in good shape. The tables need wiped off, but I doubt there will be much for us to do."

I dried my hands on a blue-checked dish towel and joined her at the table. "If you don't mind, I'm going to go with Zach in the morning and talk with his students about tips and tricks to take better outdoor photographs. We're hiking to a couple of the waterfalls in DuPont Forest. I plan to be home by three or four. He's meeting the kids at eight in the morning."

"Great idea." She slipped her shoe on. "What were you up to this morning?"

Yesterday evening, I had filled her in on Leo's birds and June's rejection. "Zach and I visited Otis's store and found notepaper and a red crayon on his counter." Uncertain whether to share about the "*reven*" word we saw, I kept it to myself.

"Why does it matter if Otis has paper and a crayon?" Her brow furrowed.

I smacked my forehead with my hand. "I didn't show you the note someone left on my car." I scrolled through the photos on my phone and showed her the one I had snapped of the note and the ones of Otis's counter. Then, I spilled about our visit to Danny.

"Lyndie, maybe Danny is right. I realize I asked you to investigate, but I don't want to place you in danger. If someone thinks you might reveal what they did, you should stop snooping." She put both feet on the floor and leaned into me. With her hands on mine, she fixed her eyes on me. "I'd never get over it if something bad happened to you."

Her soft skin wrapped around my hands. The crow's feet around her eyes reminded me she'd grown older over the years. The last thing I wanted to do was hurt my aunt, but I was so close to figuring out the truth. "I understand, and I'll be super careful. I lived through much more dangerous circumstances in the last twenty years. Please don't worry about me. Pray I find answers."

"You're as stubborn as your dad, but I respect you wanting to do the right thing." She stood and drew me into a tight hug. "Of course, I'll pray for you." She released me. Tears dampened my eyes from the gratitude I held for my aunt.

"You've no idea how much I appreciate you." I patted her cheek.

"Walt's bringing dinner. Want to help me finish the laundry? I hung the sheets on the clothesline early this morning after you stripped the beds and washed them."

"Sure." I trailed her out the back door to the clothesline where two sets of white sheets and pillowcases, dotted with pink flowers, flapped in the breeze. The scent of fresh sheets from the line beat any artificial fabric softener. Side-by-side we unclipped the pins and tossed them into a miniature apron-shaped holder made from nineteen thirties fabric. Aunt Cordy had told me the clothespin holder had belonged to her granny.

"Since these are going back on the beds, I'm not challenging myself by trying to fold the fitted sheets." Instead, I rolled them and dropped them into the basket.

She laughed. "I don't blame you."

I huffed into the house and up the steps with the laundry basket. After a tug-of-war with the fitted sheets and a smoothing out of the top ones, I finished with the pillows and bedspreads. I sat on my bed to take a breather, and my phone chimed.

"Hello."

"Miss Lavender, I want to speak to you." A woman's voice sounded in my ear.

"Who is this?" The caller ID appeared to be from an unknown caller.

A cough came through the phone. After a ragged inhale, the woman spoke. "Please don't try to find the person who killed your mayor. That person is my friend, and I want you to stop. The reason they did what they did was for me." Her cough rattled my phone.

"Who are you? How did you know the mayor?" Was there a way to trace her call?

"It doesn't matter who I am. What matters is for you to stop searching for the person who did it." Another cough came over the phone.

"You sound like you're very sick. Can I help you?" The cough rattled from her lungs.

"The only way you can help"...she gasped..."is to leave my friend alone." With a click, she hung up.

I stared at my phone. Who was the caller and her friend? How did she get my number?

Chapter Twenty-Four

The fresh scent of the sheets brought no comfort. The pink walls of the bedroom pushed in against my anxious, pounding heart. I attempted to breathe, but only gasped. My left arm ached as if a vice squeezed it, and my head pounded. I patted the bedspread five times, counted four books on my bed stand, listened to a bird singing outside, then brushed my hand over the bed in hopes my senses calmed my panic. Not PTSD, but a panic attack. They hit me less often now but when I least expected.

I lay down on top of my fresh bed and studied the hand-stomped ceiling. My aunt loved the retro vibe and had kept the house the way I remembered it from high school. I breathed deep and my heartbeat calmed. I closed my eyes and let my breath flow in and out.

A tap on my bedroom door startled me out of sleep. "Lyndie. Are you okay?" Aunt Cordy stood in my doorway. "Walt brought dinner, and Zach is here."

"I dozed off. Being out in the fresh air today made me sleepy." A foggy memory plucked at my brain. Had I received a phone call from a woman ill with respiratory problems, or did I dream it? "I'll be down in a few minutes. Let me freshen up." AKA, I wanted to check my phone before going downstairs.

"All right, honey. Come when you're ready." She turned, and I listened to her footsteps descend to the kitchen.

Once I knew she was out of sight, I opened my recent calls, and sure enough, a phone number I didn't recognize glared at me. The time matched the time I finished making the beds. I'd have to share this with Danny. It was too important to keep to myself. After I went to the bathroom and washed my face, I headed to dinner.

The fragrance of fried chicken made my stomach grumble. Sometimes a panic attack stole my appetite, but not this time. The tater salad, rolls, and green beans drew me in. I tucked into the table beside Zach. "Wow, Walt. This smells amazing. Thank you."

"Happy to bring you all a treat. Renee made the food fresh when I ordered. I can't resist the fried chicken. Best in the south, if you ask me." He patted his belly. "I blame her for these extra fifteen pounds."

Aunt Cordy grinned at Walt. "I can imagine it's hard to live in town without eating food from The Gathering Place once in a while."

Zach touched my hand, and I jumped. He pulled away. "I'm sorry. I thought we held hands when we prayed here."

Aunt Cordy watched me. "We do. Are you okay, Lyndie?" She kept her eyes on me.

"Um... can we talk about it after dinner? I'm hungry."

"Sure." She nodded to Walt. "Want to ask the blessing?"

After Walt's brief prayer, Zach passed me the chicken, and I snagged a leg and thigh. My favorites. We filled our plates and dove in.

"How are Floss and Thimble these days?" Walt inquired about my pets.

I finished a bite of my buttery roll. "They're wonderful. I appreciate so much you thinking of me when their owner moved. They help me stay calm. Plus, they love Bashful and Happy. I see them frolic around the field together. I ordered a few books through Janine's store to learn more about their care. There aren't many books on the subject." How long could I discuss the care of Valais Blacknose sheep before I had to answer questions? Not long enough. We cleaned the table and tossed or recycled containers and gathered in the living room with coffee and chocolate chip cookies from Delight's bakery. My aunt had warmed them in the microwave, and the sweet smell of chocolate and pecans preceded her into the room.

We all chose a cookie, then Aunt Cordy eyed me. The time had come to spill the story.

"Okay. After I finished making the beds, I received a phone call." I paused and sipped my coffee and hoped it was decaf.

"And?" Zach bounced his knee.

I placed the cookie on a napkin and rested my coffee cup on a nearby table. "A woman, who wheezed and coughed on the phone, begged me to stop investigating the mayor's murder. She said her friend had a reason to do what they did. She didn't indicate if the culprit was male or female." I pinched my nose beneath my glasses. "I felt bad for her. She coughed and had a raspy voice. Sure wish I had had a way to record her." I reached for my cookie and bit into it.

Zach tapped his fingers on the arm of the chair. "Did you notice an accent or any background noise?"

"Are you sure you aren't a detective?" Walt chuckled.

Zach raised his hand in front of him. "You couldn't pay me enough to snoop as a professional."

"I'm sure Danny would love your description of his job." Aunt Cordy chuckled this time.

"I need to share this with Danny. It's beyond me." I turned to Zach. "Want to take me to Danny and Laurel's house? I'll text first to see if they're home. The kids may have had a soccer game today."

"Sure. It's only six." He tipped his coffee cup to his mouth.

What a great guy. I tapped out a message and, in a few minutes, received a response. "She said, come on over."

"You kids go on, and Walt and I will pray over the situation. What a strange turn of events." She shooed us out the door.

Outside, I pointed to my Jeep. "Let's drive her tonight." I handed him the keys.

"You want me to drive your baby?" He jingled the keys.

"Yes." We both climbed in, and he started the Jeep and steered out of the driveway. "I might as well tell you. The phone call caused a panic attack. That's why my aunt found me asleep. They suck the life out of me, so to speak. I didn't come home with PTSD like some of my colleagues. Instead, I carried home anxiety and panic attacks. They're manageable with my meds and lots of prayer, but once in a while something triggers me, and I experience heavy breathing and heart palpitations, plus a headache. It stinks, but it's part of my life now."

"I'm so sorry you have to deal with those. Do you feel better now?" We reached the outskirts of town.

"Yeah. The nap helped. If I can lie down and rest, it settles me." In a few minutes, we pulled in front of Laurel's home. Zach opened my door. He was quick, or I was slow. Either way, I appreciated his gesture. Josephine opened the front door. She curtsied as if she were a princess and gestured for us to enter her kingdom. Inside, she and Henry hugged me. Nothing beat hugs from my niece and nephew to settle my nerves.

Laurel guided us to the screened-in porch. They had added the porch to the back of the house as a three-season room with glass windows to close during the chillier weather. Today, the view of their backyard wonderland made me smile. Danny had built a fort connected to a tree house for the kids. A small swinging bridge connected the fort to the tree, and a ladder ran up to the top of the trunk. The kids spent hours there pretending to be pirates, princes, and princesses. Danny even attached a doggie door for their corgi, Elizabeth. Betty for short. I watched Josephine and Henry cross the swinging bridge to the tree. "They have so much energy. Wish I could borrow some."

"You and me both." Laurel chimed. "So, what's going on? Danny will be here in a minute. He wanted to take a shower."

"I'll tell you when I tell him."

"Tell me what?" Danny ran a hand through his damp hair as he perched on a chair across from me. "Has something else happened?"

Zach sat beside me on a metal glider and rocked the seat back and forth. Laurel had inherited Aunt Cordy's love for vintage. She had collected the furniture for the porch from yard sales and refurbished the pieces.

I held my phone up. "I received a weird phone call today." In the next fifteen minutes, I explained the call. "The voice sounded like a woman with distressed breathing. It freaked me out." No way I was telling Laurel and Danny about the panic attack. Not because I was embarrassed, but because I knew they'd make me stop investigating, which was not happening. More than anything, I wanted to find the killer.

"I don't suppose you recorded it?" Danny held out his hand. "Can I see your phone?"

I handed it to him. "I didn't think I could record it."

He poked around on my cell, then wrote in his ever-present notepad. "Bring your phone to the station tomorrow. I want to see if we can get any useful information." He handed the device back to me. "I'm going to say this one more time, even though it won't help. You need to stop investigating. You're obviously getting close to figuring out who killed the mayor, and this person wants you to stop."

"She sounded so desperate, like the person she wanted to protect meant a lot to her." I slid my phone into my pants pocket, then I shivered as if someone ran an ice cube along my spine. What if the killer didn't mean to murder the mayor, but wanted to hurt him enough...to what? "Do you think the mayor's murder was an accident?"

"Since you won't stop asking questions, I might as well tell you." Danny slid his socked feet from under his chair. "There's a likely chance the person who hit the mayor with the apple butter paddle didn't think he'd die. The way the mayor landed on the sharp limestone block caught him in the neck at the wrong angle, and there's no way he would have lived. Whether the person who swung the paddle meant Mayor Richardson more harm than a bump on the head, we won't find out until we catch them. Either way, they caused someone to die, so we have to do due diligence. If you insist on continuing your investigation..." Danny cleared his throat. "Please keep me posted. Stop by tomorrow with the phone. I won't be in the office until after noon."

"I'll bring the phone in after three. Zach is teaching a class in the morning, and I'm teaching photography tips." I relaxed against the glider's back.

Josephine and Henry scurried across the swinging bridge from the tree house to the fort. Danny had added turrets with windows. Josephine poked her head out of the window on one side and Henry on the other. Life had been simple as a kid.

Zach pointed at the kids' play fort. "Danny, Lyndie told me you built the play set. It's impressive. I'd love to try building some small pieces of furniture once I get more established here.

My grandpa and I used to make wooden toys to give away at Christmas."

Danny rose from his seat. "Want a tour?"

"He loves opportunities to show off his handiwork." Laurel winked at her husband.

Zach and Danny walked to the backyard. Laurel joined me on the glider. "I was hoping I'd get a minute alone with you. Are you okay? The call had to shake you."

"I'm good, and yes, it rattled me. She sounded so pitiful and so ill. I wanted to ask if I could help her or send her help, but all she wanted was to protect the person she called about." My eyes stung.

Laurel held my hand. "You won't stop until you discover the truth, and Danny told me he doesn't want me involved because of the kids, but if I hear anything, I'll tell you."

"Thanks." I squeezed her hand. "One question that keeps rolling in my mind is, how did she get my phone number?"

Chapter Twenty-Five

The glider swooshed under us as Laurel and I pushed back and forth. Danny and Zach stood in the grass and examined the swinging bridge as the sun set, and shadows fell across the yard. A cool breeze flowed through the screen and gave me a shiver.

Laurel stared at me.

"What?" I raised my hands in question.

"It's my fault she found your number." She shook her head, then lifted her phone from the table beside her. She scrolled with her finger, then held the device to my face.

At the bottom of Laurel's website, she had added *Photos by Lyndie Lavender* plus my phone number in case anyone wanted to contact me to take photographs. She had asked my permission, and I had said, "What a great idea." Not sure about the idea now.

"Do you want me to take it off?" She wore our mom's frown when something went wrong, and she felt bad.

"Of course not. It's there for a reason, and she must have found it on the site. It's all right. Maybe she'll call back, and I'll be better prepared."

Josephine and Henry bounded onto the porch. "Aunt Lyndie, can we show you something?"

"Sure." I stood, then followed them to the treehouse. Inside, I ducked my head and watched the two of them pull a well-loved sheet off of something.

"What have you two been doing?" They stood in front of what they had uncovered.

Josephine clasped her hands in front of her. "We've been working on a spy machine." They moved apart and held their hands out to point me to their invention. They had cut a door in a cardboard box as tall as the ceiling. I wasn't sure how they got it inside the treehouse, but there it stood. "Walk through the magic door."

Henry took my hand and led me inside. "Sit on the chair." I squatted on a child's chair. A telescope stood in front of me, pointing out the cut-out window. A low table beside the chair held a notebook and a jar of pens and pencils, plus a magnifying glass. "Look through the telescope, Aunt Lyndie."

I peered through the lens. My view took in the community park behind their house. I turned the telescope to the left and caught sight of Marcy Fox and Johnson Winters. They appeared cozy. Johnson held Marcy's hand as they walked and chatted. Too bad I couldn't hear them. Before I got carried away, I sat back.

"What do you think?" My niece grinned.

"This is interesting. Have you told your mom you're spying on people in the park? Or your dad?" I held out my arms to them, and they let me hug them.

"Nope. We want to be like you. We heard you talking to Mom about catching the person who hurt the mayor." My nephew nodded as he spoke.

Oh, dear. My sister's response wouldn't be good, nor Danny's. He'd give me a tongue-lashing for sure. My tummy fell to my feet and swirled as if a sink emptied down a drain. "Listen, I appreciate you wanting to be like me, but it's not polite to spy on innocent people. How about you use the telescope to watch birds or stars and keep a notebook of what you discover? You'd be spying on nature. Wouldn't that be more fun?" I prayed they'd listen.

Josephine tapped her mouth with her finger. The wheels in her young brain rotated. "Thanks, Aunt Lyndie." She scribbled out the title *Spying on Park People* and changed it to *Spying on Beautiful Birds and Stellar Stars.*

I hugged my two favorite young humans. "You might see some butterflies too."

"I hope so." Henry fist-bumped me.

I left them to play their games and search the trees for birds, while I walked to the porch where Zach and Danny had joined Laurel. In a last effort to glimpse Johnson and Marcy, I craned my neck and peered over the fence. Their heads leaned close together. Were they an item now?

"Hey, Sis. What are you gawking at?" My sister caught me. I couldn't hide anything from her.

I settled on the glider beside Laurel, indecisive about whether to share what the kids had said about me. Did I want Danny to give me grief, or did I let it go and hope my niece and nephew listened? Might as well spill. "Your darling children wanted to show me their spy machine. They have a telescope set up toward the park. They said they wanted to be like me and spy on people."

"Seriously?" Danny ran his hand through his hair and shook his head.

I held my hand out in a stop-sign motion. "Hang on. I suggested they study birds and butterflies instead, and the stars. They agreed with me when I explained how rude it was to watch innocent people."

Laurel held her hand over her heart. "Thank goodness. They better listen to you."

"They changed the title on their notebook to reflect the conversation. I hope it sticks." My nephew and niece didn't need to get into trouble because of me. "As far as gawking. I noticed Johnson and Marcy as they walked hand in hand through the park."

"Sounds like he's sweet on her. I've seen him working on the building behind her shop. It appears he's fixing it up. Does she own it?" Laurel's gaze skirted around me as she stared at the park.

"I saw him there yesterday when I drove through town." Zach rocked in one of the white wooden rockers Aunt Cordy had gifted to Laurel and Danny. "Marcy held the ladder for him."

"Danny, who owns the building?"

He squinted at me, then rose from his chair and opened the screen door. "Hang on." He let the wooden frame slap behind him. Laurel scrunched her eyebrows and glared after him.

After a few minutes of us waiting in silence, he carried his phone to the porch and took his seat. Then he tapped on the screen of his phone.

He lifted his face from the phone to us. "I'm checking the auditor's website." His eyes focused on the phone. "Here we go. You aren't going to believe this. Otis Reardon owns the old place. No wonder the mayor refused to allow Marcy to repair it and use it for expansion. He didn't want Otis to benefit from renting to Marcy."

"What?" Laurel's hand flew to her mouth. She stared at Danny and let her hand drop to her lap. "Were you aware he owned the old, dilapidated shack?"

Danny scratched his head, then eyed Laurel. "No. I had no idea or reason to find out." He stared into space. "Otis must be renting it to Marcy. Then he benefits from Winters renovations."

Zach stopped rocking. "Mayor Richardson may have used it as a playing chip with Otis. He didn't appear to get along with the man, and if he controlled what buildings might or might not be restored in town, he rubbed his control in Otis's face."

I stood and then paced the screened-in porch before I stopped in front of Zach. "What you said makes sense."

Laurel bit her lip before she spoke. "What if all three of them were in cahoots to get rid of the mayor?"

"It's possible." I stood with my hands on my hips, like my mom when she worked through a decision. "Zach. Want to take me home?"

"Sure." He stood beside me. "I'm going home and see if I can find anything about Johnson Winters on my computer." Before Danny told me not to, I turned to him. "I promise I'll be careful. I won't do anything to alert him or anyone else to what I'm doing."

Danny rose to tower over me. "We've done a background check on him, and he has no priors."

"Okay. Then I shouldn't find anything suspicious." I waved my fingers and bounded to the car before my brother-in-law stopped me.

Zach wound out of town to Aunt Cordy's. Peace had settled over the homestead before the crowded, hectic pace of the festival on Saturday. Thimble, Floss, Happy, and Bashful poked their noses through the fence. Murphy rested beside the fence in the grass. A sweet calm settled over me as I approached those adorable creatures. With Zach on my heels, I made my way to the gate, and we found ourselves surrounded by cuteness.

I ran my hands through their fleece, then checked the water and feed, while the goats danced around Zach. Inside their shed, I plopped onto the bench, exhausted from the tension of trying to figure out who killed the mayor. Why did I think I had to solve the case? To prove to Danny I could? To catch the person who took someone's life? To relieve my aunt's guilt because it happened on our property, or because I needed a puzzle to solve? I loved life on the farmstead, but I missed being alert to my surroundings and dodging danger in my former job.

Zach's warm hand rested on my shoulder. "Are you okay? You were mumbling to yourself." He lowered himself onto the bench.

"I'm sorry. I had a moment of doubt about why I should keep trying to solve this awful mystery." I leaned my head in my hands and stared at the straw-covered floor. "It's been two weeks, and I'm not any closer than I was."

"Neither is Danny." His words rang through the little building.

I took his face in my hands and planted a kiss on his cheek. "You're right. I've got to keep trying."

Zach's eyes widened, and his mouth fell slack.

"Oh, my goodness. I didn't mean to kiss you...er...or...your cheek." My face flamed hot. The heat flushed up my neck and onto my cheeks. "I'm so happy you pointed out that Danny hasn't figured it out either. I want him to, I do, but I have to keep trying too."

He rubbed his cheek. "I understand. Glad I could help." A faint smile rested on his lips.

After an embarrassing few seconds, we hiked out of the gate, locked it, and then tramped to the house.

I turned to him on the porch. "Want to help me?"

He pushed his glasses up the bridge of his nose. "Sure. I guess."

He hesitated because he thought I was crazy. In the short time I'd known him, I got it. I'd been a woman on a mission to find a killer. "Great. Let's dig into Johnson Winters and Mayor Richardson and see what we can find on our computers to make these two men more transparent."

"Let me grab my laptop from the cabin, then I'll meet you here." He pointed to the rockers on my aunt's porch.

Fifteen minutes later, Zach and I opened web browsers. "I'm going to search for information on Mayor Richardson, if you'll try to find what you can on Johnson Winters."

He nodded, and we tapped on our keyboards. Cardinals chirped in the background, and a light breeze ruffled my hair. Jasper had shared how Mayor Richardson used the name Happy Richards when the mayor lived in and ran a business in Charleston. I typed the name and city into the search engine. Sure enough, a photo of him with more hair appeared on the screen. He'd opened a bail bonds business. How interesting. I typed in Richard Hap to widen the search and paused when I found an engagement photo of a much younger Mayor Richardson with a woman, his fiancé I assumed. Except the name attached to the photo said Richard Hapman. I held my laptop screen closer to my face to make sure I was seeing the mayor. A newspaper article linked him to a small town in the state of Washington. The mayor told us he'd never married.

The article named the woman as Bell Parker, daughter of Joseph and Lily Parker. I'd started down an interesting rabbit hole. I'd follow the rabbit as long as I found viable information.

I'd forgotten Zach rocked beside me. He tapped my arm.. "Did you find something?"

My head jerked back. "I believe I did. You're going to want to read this."

Chapter Twenty-Six

Daylight dimmed and the evening air chilled me, and goosebumps covered my arms. Aunt Cordy pushed the screen door open and handed me a flannel shirt.

"I heard you two out here and figured you might be chilly. I'm hoping this doesn't bring rain on Saturday. We're due for a sprinkle tomorrow." She rubbed her shirtsleeves.

I slipped into the soft flannel. "Thank you. Short sleeves were fine earlier in the day, but the cloud cover dropped the temperature." My aunt slid onto the swing. "We're researching Johnson Winters and the mayor."

"Do you want to come to the table? Might be more comfortable, and I can fix you sandwiches." She raised her eyebrows as if to say use some common sense. She made her point. Zach and I both rose to go inside.

We settled at the scarred kitchen table, where many memories lived. Zach opened his laptop and clicked through some pages. "Look at this." He pivoted his device so I could view the screen. A photo of Johnson Winters with a woman stared back at me. The lady allowed him to hook his arm around her shoulders. I'd seen her face before, but where?

"This is Johnson with his best friend. It popped up on a social media page, but his name is Jack Winterby. I typed in J. Winter* and stumbled across him. Why the change of name?" We studied the photo. "He's younger and has more brown in his hair than gray, but I'm certain it's him."

"Where was the photo taken? Is there a tag showing the place?" I leaned in and studied the background.

Zach clicked more keys. "A small town in Washington state. Pretty far from here." He enlarged the photo. "The caption says, 'best friends forever.' Her face tells me she's not happy."

"He's friendlier than she's comfortable with. Can you find a name for the woman?"

We both focused on our computers and continued to scroll.

"You two ready for a break?" Aunt Cordy handed us each a plate with pimento cheese sandwiches, chips, and apple slices.

"My stomach says I'm ready. I haven't eaten in a while." I bit into the sandwich. "Delicious. Your pimento cheese spread is the best. You should sell it at the festival."

"Too much work to sell. I'd rather make it for family." She joined us at the oak table. "What do you think, Zach?"

Around a mouth full of food, he responded. "Good. Great." He wiped his mouth with a napkin. "Sorry. It's the best cheese sandwich I've ever eaten. My mom made cheese spread, but she added olives. I'm not a fan. This is perfect."

Aunt Cordy wrinkled her nose. "I'm not an olive eater either, but Lyndie could eat a whole jar."

"Only in Greece. They're amazing there. I got to experience an olive farm and watch the process of how they made olive oil, and I ate the olives they brined. If you haven't tried the real thing, you haven't experienced an olive. We ate them with feta cheese or with bread for breakfast." A jolt of sorrow grabbed me by surprise. I had traveled to Greece with Elias and three other photographers for a respite. We'd enjoyed every minute. The memories brought an ache and gratitude.

"Lyndie, I found the name of the woman." Zach wrote in the notebook Lyndie had placed on the table. He turned it for me to read.

"Rinda Trent. Never heard of her." I stared at her photo on the laptop. "The photo is blurry, but her face is familiar."

Aunt Cordy leaned over our shoulders. "I've seen her face in the mayor's office on his credenza. He kept several photographs of the pets he'd had through the years, but this one sat in the corner, behind the photo of his German shepherd. I wouldn't have noticed except I had to wait on him one day."

"Me too. I was there to talk to him about the possibility of doing photography work for the town, and I had to wait." I leaned closer to the screen. "Was there anyone else in the photo with her?"

"I don't think so. I remember seeing a photo of an Irish setter. The dog may have been with her."

I leaned back in the chair. "We have more digging to do."

"While you dig, I'll make tea." My aunt's knack for caring for her people wrapped me in a warm hug.

Ten minutes later, the teakettle whistled on the stove. Aunt Cordy poured hot water over lavender-infused decaf tea. She opened the honey jar and added a teaspoon to each cup with a dollop of milk. One of my favorite evening treats. She carried the tea to Zach and me, then plated her lemon bars and tempted us with them.

"I'm going to gain ten pounds hanging around you two." Zach lifted a bar cookie from the Melmac plate, then sunk his teeth into the sugary goodness. He swallowed with a smile on his face. "Ten pounds isn't so bad, right?"

Laughter filled the kitchen and released tension in my shoulders. I bit into the lemon treat and let myself relax for a minute. Not too long, though. I continued to search and type. "How did Mayor Richardson and Johnson Winters, or whoever they are, connect to the lady in the photo? Do you think the mayor lived in Washington?"

Jasper Blake had shared he had met the mayor in Charleston and instead of Arthur Richardson, he went by Happy Richards. My fingers clattered on the keys as I typed Happy Richards into the laptop. Several sources filled the screen. "Hey, we can get happy and rich in two weeks."

"What?" Zach leaned over to see the screen. "I typed in the name Jasper told me. The first link is a get-rich-quick scheme. Wait, here's an article about the Happy Construction Company. It names Happy Richards as the owner." I moved the laptop for Zach and Aunt Cordy to see.

"A younger version of the mayor." My aunt shook her head. "Why did he lie to us?"

I glanced over the article. "He had some trouble with his inspections and had to pay fines for cutting corners." I scrolled to another article. "In this one, he won an award, but in the next one, he filed for bankruptcy." Down the page, a photo of the mayor and another woman caught my attention. "Marcy Fox?"

Zach stood behind me. "Sure looks like her."

"So, Marcy had spent time with the mayor when he was Happy Richards. Interesting. I'd think she could have used the leverage to get the building next door to her renovated and gain more space." I rubbed my temples. "Our little town has some secrets."

Zach sat in his chair then took a swig of tea. "Shouldn't we share this with Danny?"

I looked over the top of my glasses at him. "I suppose, but I want to talk to Marcy first. Could be she had a good reason to keep her relationship with Mayor Richardson quiet. They appear pretty friendly in the photo. He's got an arm wrapped around her waist, and she's leaning into his shoulder. They're on a beach. See the ocean in the background?" I tapped my fingernail against the screen. "If she knew the mayor so well, why didn't she expose him when he came to Seldom Seen? She's lived here for years, hasn't she?"

Aunt Cordy turned from the sink where she rinsed the kettle. "She grew up here. Graduated three years ahead of Laurel. I've never been close friends with her. She's held herself to a different standard than I do. Too fussy for me. She moved away for a few years, then returned and opened her shop."

Aunt Cordy had abandoned her modeling days at a Charleston department store and embraced the simple life on the homestead with my uncle. Her desire to live a life without drama or competition with the neighbors inspired me. I loved her heart to help others and embrace God's creation.

Zach yawned and his eyes drooped from lack of sleep.

"How about we finish our search tomorrow?" I rubbed my forehead.

He covered his mouth with his hand and then nodded. "Sounds good." He snapped his laptop closed.

"Aunt Cordy, do you need me to help tomorrow with festival preparations? I want you to have a good take on the last day." I closed my laptop.

She leaned her arms on the back of a kitchen chair. "If you could help me tomorrow evening, I'd appreciate it. The tables need wiped down again, and I want to inventory what I have left."

"Sounds good. In the morning, I'm going with Zach to his workshop, then on a hike, but I'll be back by early afternoon." I touched Zach's hand. "I'll drive myself to make sure I get back in time, but I want to follow you, so I don't get lost."

"Perfect." We both rose from the table.

I walked Zach to the door. "Thanks again for your help. I know you have other things to do."

"I don't mind. The only other thing I do is work. Helping to solve a mystery is exciting, although I don't want to do this too often." His smile reached his bloodshot eyes. Even in his tired state, he pushed through.

"Me too. I'm not fond of tracking down a killer, but I can't stop." We stepped onto the porch. "Night."

He jumped off the bottom step and veered in the direction of his cabin.

I popped my head back inside the door. "I'm going to go see the sheep before I go to bed."

"Okay. I'll leave the door unlocked." My aunt stood at the bottom of the steps. "I'm heading to bed. Tell those two I love them."

"I sure will." I closed the door and skipped down the steps. Before I visited the field and their shed, I slid the barn door open. Inside, I flicked on a light and hiked across the expanse to the sheep's feed. The barrel stood empty, so I cut open a fresh bag, hefted it to my shoulder, and then poured it in. After I filled the container, I shoved the lid on tight. Straw had scattered across the floor when I'd carried it out earlier. I tracked down a broom and swept the straw into the corner to pick up later. As I straightened supplies on a shelf, a chill crawled along my spine, and my brain snapped to alert. I slid behind the barrel I had filled and let my eyes wander over the barn's interior. Something jumped at me. I let out a scream like a little girl throwing a tantrum. In front of me stood a cat. Yep, a cat. A big, black, green-eyed barn cat. I'd seen the creature lurking around the barn a few days ago but had forgotten about it. My heart pounded until I took a few breaths in and out and my pulse slowed. I approached the animal, and she scatted away. I scared her as much as she startled me. Hand on my chest, I sat on a folding chair we kept in the barn. Once the thump of my heart slowed, I rose, closed the barn door, then tramped to the field.

As soon as my sweet sheep came into view, I calmed. They had no idea how much I needed them. I wanted my shepherd with me every day, and I'm sure my sheep felt the same. Now, I longed to sit with them, share my day, and run my hands through their fleece.

Inside the shed, they nuzzled my legs. I knelt between them and wrapped my arms around their necks. "Guys, it's been a long day. You'll never believe what we found today." I told them the story of the mayor and Marcy. They listened well. As I reiterated what we found, I forged a plan.

At the festival, I'd find out more about the two of them and Johnson Winters. Was he playing Marcy? I'd hate to see her hurt, but what if she was involved in the mayor's death? I'd chat with Zach, Aunt Cordy, Danny, and Laurel tomorrow evening. They'd be at the house setting up for Saturday.

I cuddled the sheep for a few more minutes, then climbed the porch steps and entered the house for a much-needed rest.

Chapter Twenty-Seven

Friday morning, I wound the Jeep Cherokee around the mountain curves behind Zach's car. Fifty-eight degrees, a few clouds, and an abundance of sunshine filled me with the desire to run along the mountain road. Instead, the Jeep climbed the steep route to the parking lot, where I slid in next to Zach.

A group of folks emerged from waiting cars and gathered around Zach after he exited his vehicle. "Good morning. Thanks for requesting a hike to Hooker Falls. It's a little steep in one place, but not difficult. I had a sixty five-year-old lady with me on the last hike, and she made it with no trouble. She wouldn't mind me sharing, since she was proud of herself."

Three ladies in their fifties giggled and adjusted their drawstring backpacks, no doubt filled with their lunches. A couple in their twenties with two children and a mom with six children clamored to follow their leader along the trail. I stepped beside Zach. "You've got a fun bunch today."

"Indeed. I enjoy when the group varies in age and experience. Most of the time they teach each other." He turned to face the group.

"I'll point out a few things along the way. Feel free to ask questions."

Loose gravel crunched under our feet as we followed Zach along the trail like a family of ducks.

After hiking for a few minutes, Zach stopped. He drew attention to knee-high, green and purple plants growing along the side of the path. Not a plant I remembered.

"Not many plants are coming to life in the fall, but the crane-fly orchid does. They grow in the forest in September and October. The green leaves have purple underneath. They winter over before they disappear in the spring. If anyone wants to photograph them, we'll wait."

Most of the hikers aimed their phones at the plant and snapped pictures, including me.

Zach led us further on the path. "On our left is Hooker-Moore Cemetery. The families who lived here before the park was installed buried family members here as well as members of a Baptist church. Interesting fact, none of the Hooker family members are buried here, but there is a Union soldier who came to visit his sister and was killed. Many of the stones are aged or flat on the ground. Let's keep going."

As we reached the crest of the hill, I heard rushing water. We turned a corner, and Hooker Falls cascaded into the river. We followed Zach across the rocky ledge, and stood close enough for the mist to touch our faces.

"The falls have about a fourteen-foot drop, and it's wider than it is high. Years ago, a grist mill operated here where they ground wheat into flour and corn into grits." The rest of Zach's words floated away on the breeze. The cemetery we passed tugged at my imagination. My eyes were fixed on the waterfall, but my mind dove into the mystery of how Johnson, the mayor, and Marcy knew each other. Something touched my arm.

"Lyndie, we're heading back to the trail." Zach dropped his hand from my arm.

On the hike back, I pondered the possibility of Marcy living in Washington before she moved to Seldom Seen. Anything was possible. When we reached the parking lot, I leaned into Zach. "If you don't mind, I'm going to go. Can I share photography tips another time?"

"Sure. I hadn't told the group you'd share tips. We have another waterfall to hike to, and I have a talk to give about Dupont Forest. I'll be back later today." He lowered his voice. "Whatever you're up to, be careful."

"I will." I hopped into my Jeep and steered toward town. When I reached Maple Street, I steered into a parking spot in front of the Foxy Glove. The sign on the door announced it as open for business. I climbed out of my car and hurried into the store. No Marcy. As a matter of fact, no one meandered around the store. Cars lined Maple Street when I drove into town. Patrons walked along the sidewalks. I guess nobody wanted to shop for nice clothes today.

I searched the store for Marcy, including the curtained dressing rooms. Her office and a storage area connected to the back of the sales room down a short hallway. When I reached the office and knocked on the door, no one answered. I turned the knob, and the door opened. No Marcy. Next, I checked the storage room. I called her name, then walked into clothing hanging on garment racks and boxes of accessories. She collected more merchandise than she would ever sell. I picked my way through the maze of boxes. My toe caught on a foot clad in a black pump that stuck out from behind a stack of hatboxes. I leaned in to see who lay sprawled on the floor. "Marcy?"

With my fingers on her neck, I detected the beat of her pulse. I patted her face, and she stirred. Her eyes fluttered open. "Are you okay?"

"What are you doing in here? Why am I on the floor?" Marcy propped herself on her elbows.

I held on to her shoulder. "Stay still. If you can sit up fine, but don't stand. I'm calling the life squad so they can check you over."

She touched her hand to her head. "My head hurts. I think I have a bump on the back." She ran her fingers over the crown of her head.

I dialed 9-1-1 and gave them the location, then bent to Marcy and touched the spot on her head. "You have a goose egg. Did you fall?"

She squinted at me. "I'm not sure. I don't think I fell." She closed her eyes. "No. Someone sneaked up on me and clobbered me from behind."

"Did you see them?" I sat on the floor beside her.

"No. Um...maybe a dark blue sleeve."

The bell on the door jingled. A minute later, my brother-in-law and the EMTs hurried in.

Danny stared at me while the squad cared for Marcy. "What are you doing here? Did you knock her in the head?"

"Of course not." How could Danny think I would hit anyone? "I came by to talk to Marcy, and this is where I found her. She doesn't remember how she ended up on the floor, whether she hit her head or someone hit her. She's got a pretty big lump on her head."

"Come out to the front of the store and I'll take your statement. You can leave when you're finished, and we'll take Marcy to the clinic." He led the way to the front counter. I spilled about what I'd witnessed, then he assured me they'd take care of Marcy.

The EMTs loaded her into the life squad and drove toward the clinic on the edge of town. I guessed they'd check her for a concussion and anything else she may have injured on the way to the floor. Something or someone had knocked her cold.

I hung out in my Jeep until Danny drove away behind the squad. He had locked the store, but I had a gut feeling I should check out the area behind the shop. The Foxy Glove, like many of the downtown shops, butted up against the walking trail with a patch of grass on either side. The river flowed on the other side of the path. Someone could have entered the back door and found her in the storage room, clobbered her with a mannequin or a wooden hanger or something, then run, but why? Nothing in the store appeared disturbed. The clothes had hung on the racks and hooks as usual, and the accessories appeared in the same places Marcy displayed them last week.

Did the culprit steal money or valuables? What if some of the jewelry wasn't the costume kind?

I checked my watch. Twelve-thirty arrived before I realized. I'd head home to help Aunt Cordy in a minute or two. Later, I'd drive to Marcy's house and check on her, and perhaps ask a few questions. I'd talk to Danny about her condition before I drove to her house, but he didn't need to be privy to my plans. I'd return in time to meet with everyone tonight. First, I'd snoop behind the store.

Out back, I moved along the trail. Behind the Foxy Glove's store, the grass beside the door appeared smashed. No footprints, but a large stick stuck out of the trash bin. I didn't touch it for fear the attacker had used it as a weapon, but I'd point it out to Danny when I saw him. No doubt the police would...

"Miss Lavender, what are you doing back here?" Officer Ashton caught me.

"I wanted to see if anything looked out of place back here." Might as well be honest.

She had a hand on each hip and a scowl on her face. "Did you find anything?"

"This large stick hanging out of the bin."

"Thanks. You can go now."

I nodded and went to the Jeep. I hoped she didn't report me to my brother-in-law.

Fifteen minutes later, back at the farm, I parked beside Walt's car and Johnson Winter's truck. What's he doing here? I hopped out and followed the sound of muffled voices to the barn. Aunt Cordy, Walt, and Johnson all stared at a beam near the roof.

"What are you looking at?" I placed a hand on each hip, my defense stance, and glanced at the ceiling.

Aunt Cordy pointed to the beam. "The bee's nest. I noticed several bees swarming around the animal's food when I came out to fill the chicken feeder. I'd not seen so many until today. Walt called Johnson to ask if he could move the hive without hurting the bees. He said he'd moved bees before, and he'd be happy to."

"How long has the hive been there? I don't remember seeing it." I studied the nest.

Aunt Cordy placed her arm around my waist. "I noticed it a couple of weeks ago but waited to see if the hive had active bees. Since I've seen so many now, I want it moved."

"Makes sense." I watched Johnson leave the barn, then return with an extension ladder and a cardboard box. Dressed in beekeeper's gear, he ascended to the hive, settled the box on the beam below the nest. He climbed to the top of the ladder where he gave the hive a gentle shake and the bees dropped into the box. I'd never observed the process of bees being moved. No doubt there were other ways to move them, but this one worked.

"Where is he taking them?" He balanced the closed box as he descended the ladder.

"The Moores have bees, and they said they'd take them. They didn't have time to move them today, so they loaned Johnson a beekeeper suit so he'd not get stung."

Johnson carried the box outside, and I followed. He tucked it under a shady tree. "What are you doing?"

He removed the beekeeper's veil, turned to me, and glared. "I have to leave the box in the shade until after dark when the bees aren't as active. I'll come back and take them to the Moores this evening." His stare pierced me.

"I've never seen the process before, so I was curious." I didn't back down under his stare. "What time did you get here today?" Did he have time to attack Marcy?

"Before you." He unzipped and stepped out of the beekeeping suit and then stalked to his truck.

My spine tingled at the idea of Johnson Winters creeping around the homestead after dark. As a suspect in the mayor's death, he gave me the creeps, but he had no motive.

Aunt Cordy tapped my shoulder, and I jumped. "I'm sorry. Are you okay?"

"Not really. I found Marcy Fox knocked out in her store. Nothing life threatening. What time did Johnson get here?" I followed my aunt and Walt to the porch.

Aunt Cordy and Walt cozied into the swing, and I chose the rocker closest to them.

"He arrived right before you." Walt stretched his arm across the back of the swing.

My heart melted at the idea of this man caring for my aunt, but I didn't have time for mushy daydreams. "He may have attacked Marcy. She didn't see anything but a blue sleeve, and she wasn't certain of that."

"Oh, dear. He seems like a hardworking man." My aunt saw the good in everyone.

"Hardworking or not, I want to find out if he hurt Marcy and why." I leaned my head against the back of the rocker. As soon as I could, I'd go check on the owner of the Foxy Glove.

Chapter Twenty-Eight

I pulled the Jeep into a parking spot in front of the police department. A cool breeze whipped my hair against my neck as I approached the entrance. With my hand ready to push open the door, I raised a prayer for wisdom as I spoke to Danny. Oh, and for him not to be mad at me.

After the amen, I shoved the door open and searched the room for my brother-in-law. The office administrator leaned her head toward Danny's office. "He's in there."

"Thanks." I wove my way around the officers' desks to his office and tapped on the door.

"Come in."

I pushed the door open and found him hunched over his desk, as usual. His endless stack of paperwork surrounded him, and his computer hummed.

"Hey, Lyndie. Have a seat." He motioned to one of the wood and leather chairs. "Thanks for helping with Marcy earlier."

"Sure. I hated finding her injured. How is she?" I crossed my leg over the other and wrapped my hands around my knee to keep from swinging it.

He placed both hands on his desk and leaned toward me. "She's home with an ice pack and a slight concussion. I'm only telling you because you called for help, and you care." He raised one side of his mouth into a half-smile.

"Any idea who hit her or why?" I sat on my hands to calm myself.

He twined his fingers together and stared at me. "The hard answer is no, but my officer found a large wooden dowel rod in her trash bin we're checking for prints. It's a stick she might have used with one of her clothes racks, and the end was broken. She may have thrown it away. Do you have a suspect? I'm sure you've considered it."

I let out a breath. "Johnson Winters has been hanging around her."

"Hanging around doesn't prove anything. Marcy is going to check the store tomorrow to see if anything is missing. In the meantime, my officers are patrolling the area on a regular basis." He shuffled some papers. "Anything else?"

His cue for me to exit. I stood. "I'll see you at the homestead tonight. We have a big day tomorrow."

He rose from his chair and opened the door for me. "Later."

I hustled out of the station. The breeze had picked up, so I hurried to the Jeep, started the engine, and then drove to Marcy's house. Her cottage sat behind a white picket fence. The small porch donned pots of lavender chrysanthemums and purple pansies. White wicker furniture with overstuffed pillows and a colorful quilt invited guests to relax. A light shone in the window, perhaps one she left on all the time. I knocked at the old-fashioned screen door, with a light touch in case she was asleep.

After a minute, Marcy squinted at me through the screen. “Hi, Lyndie. Come in.” She moved to the side to allow me to pass.

Inside, the house shouted shabby chic. A set of white bookshelves filled the wall behind a pale pink couch, decorated with floral pillows. Candles and vintage dishes mingled with old books in cloth covers. Tasteful, gauzy curtains graced the windows. The decor created a sophisticated coziness.

Marcy led me to an overstuffed chair upholstered in robin’s egg blue and white chintz fabric. She rested on the couch.

I sank into the chair and crossed my ankles. “How are you?”

She lifted a cloth ice bag. “This and some pain meds have helped. My head has pounded since I got home, but it’s better now. The doctor said I had a slight concussion, so I should be back to work tomorrow. I’m not sure I want to go back to the place I got knocked out, but life must go on.” She shrugged deeper into the couch. “You found me, didn’t you? Thanks for your help.”

I had to admire Marcy for wanting to move forward. “You’re welcome. I’m glad I came when I did. Do you have any idea if someone hit you, or did you fall and knock your head into a shelf or table?”

She held the ice on her head. “Someone hit me. I’d gone to the storage room to get a display piece for a necklace. I was digging through a box, and next thing I remember is lying on the floor, and you hovering over me." Her eyes locked with mine. "You didn't clunk me over the head, did you?"

I held my hand to my heart. "Of course not. I wouldn't hit you or anybody else."

"Of course not, but who did?" She lay back on the couch and rested her head on the ice bag.

"You mentioned something about a dark blue sleeve." I hoped the comment might jog her memory.

She rubbed her forehead. "Yeah. I might have seen a sleeve."

"Have you made anybody mad, or is there something in the store someone might want?" What if she angered Johnson or Otis. Capable of violence? At least I thought they were?

"You're beginning to sound like your brother-in-law." She closed her eyes.

I pulled a pillow from behind my back onto my lap. On the bookshelf, a framed photo caught my eye. I rose from the chair, still holding the pillow, and walked to the shelf. A photo of Marcy and Johnson sat between a copy of *Jane Eyre* and *Little Women*. They stood in front of the waterfall I'd visited this morning. Smiles spread across both of their faces. He had his arm wrapped around her waist.

"You caught me. Johnson and I have been dating." Marcy swung her legs around and sat on the edge of the couch. "He's kind to me and has helped me with some projects at the store."

I moved to the couch and sat beside her. "Like the building next door? I heard he's renovating it. Did you buy it? Or did Otis rent it to you?"

She wrung her hands. "Otis said if we updated the building, he'd rent it to me. Johnson volunteered to repair it and paint both inside and outside."

I patted her back. "You should lie down." I crossed the room and scooted my backside into the soft cushions of the comfy chair. "Do you trust Otis to follow through?" He had a reputation for taking the upper hand while holding out a greedy hand in every situation. Whatever horrible experience had added bitterness to his life, had also left him a grumpy old man.

Marcy wiped at her eyes. "I need to rest. I'm getting weepy, and my head hurts."

I pushed myself out of the comfortable cocoon. "Of course. Can I get you anything before I leave?"

"No, I'm good." She stretched her legs.

"I'll talk to you later. Take care." I let myself out.

On the drive home, I wound my way along the gravel road we lived on. Lush, wooded areas showed off their fall rainbow of colors. My heart overflowed with gratitude for my aunt and her home. She'd welcomed me and allowed me to heal from the torments of war. Now I stood on the cusp of solving the mystery of the mayor's demise. My strength and wisdom came from God, because my body, mind, and soul had arrived at my aunt's house exhausted.

As the leaves performed their autumn dance, I pondered Marcy's situation. My gut didn't trust Otis or Johnson, although Otis had run a successful business in town for years. Sure, he'd created some enemies because of his gruff personality, and he held people responsible for paying their tab, which was a good business practice. He appeared to get along with Marcy, and I'm certain he chose to allow her to rent it and extend her shop to spite the mayor, even though he was dead.

What about Johnson Winters? Did he simply enjoy Marcy's company and want to please her? Did he have more serious intentions toward her or was he taking advantage of her relationship with Otis, in case the grumpy hardware store owner won the mayor's office? The biggest question that nagged me was, who killed the mayor?

My tires rolled onto the homestead's driveway. I glanced at the clock radio in the Jeep. Four thirty, good I had time to check on the sheep and relax a minute before everyone else arrived for supper. Aunt Cordy had invited Laurel, Danny, and their kids, plus Walt, and Zach to share a meal and finish preparations for the last day of the festival. We'd been blessed with little rain and warm days. Of course, we'd be praying for rain after tomorrow.

I parked my Jeep behind the barn and meandered to the fenced-in field and shed where my darlings lived. Between them and the goats, they kept the grass short. Before I reached the gate, the baas met my ears. I swore they grinned at me. Happy and Bashful hopped from one side to the other, and Floss and Thimble trotted to meet me. I loved dogs, but there's something about bouncing fleece I adored. The small horns poking out above their ears and those sweet black faces filled my heart with joy.

After I walked into my creatures' dwelling place, I latched the gate and knelt in front of them. "I need you two to help me solve this case." I scratched my head. "Those are words I never dreamed I'd say, but here I am. Marcy has a concussion, and I suspect it's connected to the mayor's murder. I watched a television show where the main character trusted his gut. I have trusted mine in many situations overseas and it hasn't failed me yet." Floss nudged me with her head as if she agreed.

Inside the sheep shed, I refreshed their feed and water, then rested on the bench. Thimble's head rested on my knee. I plunged my hands into her plush soft fleece. Stress left my shoulders as I held on to the plush fleece. "Thank you, Thimble." Like a therapy dog, my sheep sensed what I needed and took care of me. Happy and Bashful chased each other around the field. They crossed the door's opening, and I laughed every time they flew past. If only I could find a way to let the cares of life drop away and play for the day. Even on my hike with Zach and his students, the murder mystery weighed on my mind. I squished the fleece under my fingers. Of all the people I had suspected, only two still stood out. Otis, who wanted to run for mayor and win, or Johnson Winters, but why? He had met the mayor in a previous life. Both of them had used fake identities at least once or twice, and they appeared connected to the same woman. None of those provided a solid motive.

"Good night, girls. Aunt Cordy is expecting me for supper. We get to clean tables and count jars of apple butter after we eat." I patted their heads and hiked out of the field. After I latched the gate, I hurried past the barn. At the corner, something leaped in front of me. My heart jumped into my throat. "Meow." The black cat with the green eyes rubbed against my legs.

"Looks like you have a new friend." Zach appeared from around the corner of the house. He knelt to pet the creeper who scared me.

"I'm not sure if he's a friend or foe. He's frightened me twice." The pounding of my heart slowed, and I bent to pet the big guy. "Hard to tell where he came from. The way he wound his way around my legs makes me think he's someone's pet. Aunt Cordy will be happy to have him if he's a good mouser. I'll ask folks at the festival tomorrow if they've lost a cat. If I don't find its owner, we'll keep it."

Zach ran his hands along the creature's back. "He's wearing a collar, but no tags or identification. It's dark gray, so hard to see."

"Good find. Maybe he'll be useful." I patted the cat's head once more before I trailed along the sidewalk to the house. The smell of my aunt's meatloaf wafted through the screen door. She surrounded the meat mixture with sliced potatoes and carrots, then added ketchup, mustard, and brown sugar sauce. One of my favorite meals and fuel for tonight's chores.

Chapter Twenty-Nine

Inside my aunt's kitchen, Walt fussed over the arrangement of plates, glasses, and silverware around the table. My aunt had laid out a vintage green, red, and white floral tablecloth, one she had dressed the table with since I was a young girl. A polished wooden bowl displayed red and yellow apples as a centerpiece. Steam rose from the green beans she cooked on the stove, a perfect complement to the meatloaf.

My stomach rumbled. "Hungry?" Three voices echoed the same word. Aunt Cordy, Walt, and Zach chuckled.

I patted my tummy. "Yep." I'd forgotten to eat lunch again. I'd missed many meals overseas, sometimes because I forgot, other times because the food supply dropped low. Most of the time, we ate well enough, if a local family took mercy on us or armed forces were stationed nearby. Since I'd arrived here, I'd eaten too much. The waist of my jeans reminded me to exercise more and eat less. Although my mom would have said I was too skinny when I arrived home.

A slam of the screen door and the pounding of running feet announced Josephine and Henry. Laurel and Danny shuffled in behind their children. "Hi, Aunt Cordy." The youngsters hugged our aunt around the waist and leaned into her. She almost toppled over.

"You two have grown more every time I see you." She held onto the back of a chair with one hand and hugged with her other. "What do you say? Let's eat."

Walt held out Aunt Cordy's chair and started a chain reaction. Danny held Laurel's, Zach pulled out mine, and even Henry got his sister's chair. After prayer, we passed the food around the table. This simple action brought tears to my eyes. My parents had instilled family time into our daily schedules. I missed my mom and dad but understood their desire to stay in Guatemala until their health or circumstances prevented it.

"This is the best meatloaf I've ever eaten." Zach shoved a second bite into his mouth. "My mom added too much onion."

My aunt beamed. "Thank you. I grow green onions to add to soup and cheese ball, but I don't cook with onions most of the time." She sliced a piece of carrot with her fork.

I cleared my throat, then stopped myself. After supper I'd share with Danny what Zach and I had discovered online. I didn't want the kids privy to information they were too young to understand. Instead, I chewed my food and enjoyed the family meal.

After supper, I washed dishes in a sink filled with suds and hot water. I handed my sister a plate to dry. "So, has Danny told you anything about the mayor's..."

"I'm not supposed to discuss anything about the mayor's murder. Danny got upset because he's afraid whoever killed the mayor might target the people investigating. He intends to protect me and the kiddos." She wiped a bowl with a red and white flowered dishtowel. "Plus, I haven't had time to think about it."

I pulled the plug in the sink and listened to the water swish down the drain. It swirled in a circle and sucked the suds down. "Your life must be difficult at times. Especially when Danny or you might be in the sights of a criminal."

She folded the dishtowel and hung it over the drainer. "I'm glad you understand."

Yes, I understood, but I'd move my information gathering to Danny. I'd pick his brain while my sister helped Aunt Cordy.

Outside, Zach and Danny shifted the tables to the middle of the yard. Thank goodness, we had had little wind this week, since most of the vendors had left their canopies in place. Without extra weight and stakes, those canopies could fly like kites.

I retrieved a wet rag from my aunt's sudsy bucket and wiped the bird bombs away. Tomorrow morning I'd check to make sure I scrubbed away all of the bird's overnight deposits. When I finished, I returned the rag and spied Danny talking to my sheep. Josephine and Henry played pirates in the tree house my aunt had Leo build when they were old enough to climb.

I moseyed across the yard and leaned on the fence next to Danny. "Pretty, aren't they?"

He leaned across the fence and patted Thimble's head. "Sure are. Soft too." He heaved a sigh. "What have you been digging into now? I'm sure you haven't stopped investigating the mayor's death."

My brother-in-law knew me too well for me to get away with casual conversation. "I want to show you what Zach and I found on the internet."

Fifteen minutes later, Danny, Zach, and I gathered around the kitchen table while Laurel and Walt helped Aunt Cordy inventory jars of apple butter and sauce. I set up my laptop for Danny to view. Even though he'd been my brother-in-law for several years, his law enforcement persona caused my nerves to twitch, especially when I wanted to show him evidence, or at least what I considered evidence.

"Look at the pictures we found." I had downloaded them to a computer file for easy access. "The mayor and Johnson Winters both used fake names, not once, but several times. They were both in the state of Washington earlier in their lives, and Marcy had met the mayor when he lived in Charleston. Plus, the mayor was engaged once, and he kept a photo of his fiancée in his office. Aunt Cordy and I both saw her picture on his credenza." I tapped on the computer screen as I spoke.

Danny leaned back in his chair. Dark smudges colored the skin under his eyes. The crow's feet at the corners of his eyes creased more than usual. "We found some similar information in our searches, but none of it points to murder. They may have lived in Washington but never crossed paths. The names could be due to hiding from a breakup or an angry boss. Granted, it's not a great idea to pretend you're someone else, but there isn't enough evidence." Danny paused and studied the flowers on the tablecloth. He raised his head and peered at me. "We questioned Johnson, and he had an excuse for everything. Said he lived in Washington from his teen years through his late fifties, then he traveled and did odd jobs to pay for his trip. He landed here because he'd found our website and saw photos of our beautiful town. I didn't buy it, but he answered all the questions with logical answers. He's either a great liar or he's telling the truth." He ran his hand through his blond locks.

"What about Otis?" Zach fingered the cloth and stared at Danny.

Danny crossed his leg over his knee and crossed his arms, signs of shutting down. "I've spoken with him several times. He swears he didn't do it, but he has no alibi. The time of the mayor's death would have been when Otis was driving home alone. No one saw him leave the property or arrive home. He could have been anywhere." He held his hand in front of him to stop my inquisition. "Before you ask, I've interviewed Marcy Fox, and she claims to have been with Johnson Winters when they left the festival. She appears smitten with him."

"I've seen them holding hands and walking together." The tension in my neck traveled to the back of my head. "Have you figured out who hit Marcy?"

"Forensics found no fingerprints except Marcy's on the stick we found. So, the short answer is no. She doesn't remember anything except a flash of navy blue, which doesn't help."

Danny leaned his elbows on the table. I placed a hand on his sleeve. "If we can help at all, I'm happy to volunteer." I eyeballed Zach.

"Me too." He tossed an apple back and forth between his hands.

Danny watched Zach for a few seconds. "You, sir, have got to be careful. You could lose your job if your boss thinks poking around in an investigation might take too much of your time or be poor public relations."

"No worries. I wouldn't jeopardize my job. I've only helped when I could and only shared with Lyndie." Zach arranged the apple on top of the others.

I patted the table with both hands. "The sun has gone down. We'd better check on the others and check if they want our help."

Outside, Henry, Josephine, Laurel, Aunt Cordy, and Walt held hands and sang camp songs. "Come join us." Aunt Cordy called over Henry's head.

Many years had passed since we had clasped hands and sung together. I planted myself between Laurel and Josephine and took their hands with a gentle squeeze. Zach grabbed Walt and Aunt Cordy's hands, and Danny held his wife and son's hands. I hadn't sung a camp song since Laurel and I had attended a Christian camp in the mountains. Josephine broke into the *Song That Does Not End*. After five rounds of it, Laurel ended it. "Is there anything else you need us to do, Aunt Cordy?"

"No, Laurel. I think we're good. We've done prep every day this week, so you all can go home and get some rest." She grinned. "If you can knock the song out of your head."

"I'm sure they'll sing it all the way home." Laurel put a hand on the back of each of her children and glanced at Danny. "You ready?"

"Sure am." He hugged Aunt Cordy. "Thanks for supper. Your meatloaf was delicious as usual." Laurel and the kids hugged her and me. "We'll see you tomorrow."

We watched as their taillights bobbed along the driveway.

"I'm next." Walt shook Zach's hand and patted my back. "See you kids tomorrow, bright and early." Aunt Cordy walked Walt to his car. No doubt, they wanted a little privacy.

"I'm heading to the cabin." Zach reached out with his arms open. Then he drew back. "Sorry. Everyone was hugging, and ..." He rolled his lip between his teeth.

"No worries. I understand. I mean, I can give you a hug if you'd sleep better." My arms hugged my middle. Not the most welcoming stance.

His eyes locked with mine, and a grin crossed his face. "I'm good, but tired, so I'll sleep better than a hibernating bear. Goodnight." He turned and hiked across the grass to his haven in the small cabin.

I climbed the porch steps and slid onto the swing. The sway of the wooden hanging bench slowed my heartbeat and gave me calm. When I was little, Laurel and I took turns swinging in a tree swing our dad had made. In Guatemala, we didn't own a swing set. Instead, Dad hung the swing from a low branch, plus he had built balance beams and wooden boxes to climb on. We'd race to the top of the hill, then run through the boxes like an obstacle course.

"Hey, Lyndie. What are you daydreaming about?" Aunt Cordy lowered herself onto the swing.

I patted her hand. "The swing and playthings dad made for us when Laurel and I lived with Mom and him in Guatemala. We loved playing outside with the village children, but I'm happy they sent us back here for high school. After the festival's over, we should try to call them. I miss them, even though I chose to live all over the world too. I long to talk to them about everyday life."

She squeezed my hand. "I'm sure Laurel wants to talk to them too. She mentioned your parents to me the other day. We haven't chatted with them since before the festival started." She stood and stretched her arms over her head. "I'm heading to bed. We'll be up bright and early in the morning." She leaned toward me and kissed my cheek.

"Love you, Aunt Cordy."

"Love you, too." She disappeared through the door.

I leaned my head back, and my mind wandered to the mayor's mystery. Two weeks had passed since the man had died. "Lord, what am I missing? What's Danny missing?"

Chapter Thirty

I rocked the swing back and forth and watched clouds drift across the full moon overhead. A chill shot through me from the cool night air. I rubbed my hands up and down my arms to warm myself as I watched headlights bounce along the driveway. Had Laurel or Walt forgotten something?

A truck drove into the barnyard. Johnson Winters rolled out of his truck and trod across the grass to the side of the barn. I'd forgotten about the bees. He had told us he'd return after dark to collect them, because they calmed at night. Now might be a good time to ask a few questions, or a bad time depending on perspective and the dark, plus I was alone.

I left the comfort of the swing and followed Johnson to the tree where he'd left the box of bees earlier. He lifted the cardboard off the ground. "Hello, Johnson. Thanks for taking care of the bees."

He jumped but kept hold of the box. "Lyndie, you scared me."

"Sorry. I was on the porch and saw you pull in." He passed me and scurried to his truck. I followed. He loaded the bees into the truck bed and tossed an old floral sheet over them.

He moved to the driver's side of the truck, opened his door, then turned to me. "I'll drop these off to the folks who sell the honey. They're anxious to get them. They told me to leave them behind their barn."

I stepped back and rested my hand on the back of the truck. A shovel handle stuck out from the back. Good, before I dove into questions, I'd spotted a weapon. "Um. I was wondering. You lived in Washington when you were younger, didn't you? Did you meet Mayor Richardson when you lived there?"

Johnson squinted his eyes, and his mouth flattened into a hard line. His hands fisted. I'd hit a nerve, but I had to get answers.

"I saw the mayor's engagement picture. Were you familiar with her too?"

He watched his toe grind into the gravel.

"Did you know Bell Parker?" I backed up a step, closer to the shovel's handle.

He raised his head and narrowed his eyes. "Bell Parker lured him away from my best friend, Rinda. She had put her life on hold for that idiot. He used Rinda for her dad's connection to the construction job he wanted, then dumped her for the socialite, Bell Parker, whose family owned most of the county we lived in. When Bell discovered he wanted property more than her, she called him on it, and he disappeared. He stomped on everyone he met. Rindy never got over the jerk. I loved her and wanted to marry her, but she never wanted me. I lost track of him for years, then he resurfaced."

I straightened my spine and lifted my chin to give the pretense of fearlessness. “Did you follow him here?”

He crossed his arms. “Not on purpose. I’d been traveling and working so I could experience new areas of the country, and I ran across his photo on social media. I called Rinda, who is dying of lung cancer, and she said let him go, but I couldn’t. He broke her heart, and she broke mine. I wanted to go home and take care of her, but I wanted revenge too.”

“So, you killed the mayor?” I patted my pocket. My hand met my phone.

“Not on purpose. I planned to tell him off and ask him to call Rinda and apologize, but he got defensive.” He raised his chin and stared at me. “I’d picked up your aunt’s paddle to take a closer look. My curiosity had peaked when I listened to her describe the apple butter making process. Then he walked past me and went behind the house. I didn’t take the time to lay the paddle down. Instead, I trailed behind him. When I confronted him, he swung a fist at me. I swung back with the paddle and hit him on the head, then he fell on the sharp end of the block and bled out. I can’t say I’m sorry.” His eyes had lost their light. “By the way, Rinda called you after I told her what I’d done. I told her to have her brother buy her a burner phone.” He let a raucous laugh loose. “Even on her deathbed, she wanted to protect me.”

“What about Marcy?” The night’s chill or the lack of regret in Johnson’s voice shook me.

"Marcy means nothing to me. She kept me entertained. I'm sorry I can't finish the building for her expansion, but I'll be out of the state before the police catch me." He reached into the truck bed and lifted the box of bees out and tossed it to me. I caught it, then I watched him climb into his truck and rip out of the driveway. Before he reached the road, I had Danny on the phone. As soon as he got off the line, Laurel called me. "Are you okay?"

"I'm fine, but now Johnson is aware that I know he killed the mayor." I carried the bees and placed them under the tree, then I paced the barnyard.

"Danny called for backup and sent out the truck's description and location. At least you told him which way he turned on the road. They'll find him."

"Thanks, Laurel. I'm going in the house and lock the doors."

"You haven't done that yet?"

"No. Here I go now." I hiked to the porch, went inside, and locked the deadbolt. "Call me if you hear anything."

Aunt Cordy stood in the hallway. "What's going on? Something woke me." She wrapped her housecoat around her.

I hugged her. "Johnson peeled out of the driveway. He confessed to me he clobbered the mayor, but says it wasn't on purpose. He meant to harm him but not kill him."

"Why?" She placed a hand on my back and led me to the couch.

"Mayor Richardson, or whoever he pretended to be, was engaged to Johnson's best friend, and he left her for the daughter of a wealthy family, and then left her too when he got caught for his greed. The best friend, who Johnson loved, is dying of cancer, and it brought back all of Johnson's anger. It was an act of love, but also an act of revenge." I sank into the cushions and pushed a pillow onto my lap.

Aunt Cordy walked to the doorway. "I'm going to make us tea."

I closed my eyes. Greed never paid, nor did revenge. I'd witnessed too much of both through the years.

*****

The cup of tea my aunt had made had cooled on the coffee table, and an afghan covered me. I rubbed my eyes, then glanced at my watch. Six o'clock in the morning stared back at me. What little light filtered through the lace curtains revealed Aunt Cordy in the recliner in the corner of the living room. On the coffee table, a light blinked at me from my cell phone.

I carried my phone and the cup of tea to the kitchen and flipped on the lights. After the microwave heated my tea, I sat at the table and opened my phone. Danny had left me a text message. *Winters has been apprehended. Thanks for the heads-up. I'll need your statement sometime today.*

Laurel had left a message a few minutes ago. *I'm coming to the homestead at seven. Danny got the jerk.*

The last message I opened was from Zach. *I saw lights on. Okay if I come over?*

I typed back. *Give me an hour. Johnson killed the mayor. Danny caught him.*

Aunt Cordy padded into the room. "Morning."

"Good morning. Danny caught him." I held my phone up.

She sank into a chair. "Thank goodness."

By seven o'clock, Laurel, Henry, Josephine, and Zach gathered around the table with us. After my niece and nephew ran outside to visit the animals, I caught everyone up on what had transpired with Johnson.

Laurel stared over her coffee cup at me then set it on the table. "You shouldn't have confronted him by yourself."

"Yeah. You're right, but I had a shovel at the ready to defend myself with." I bit into an apple muffin and considered my sister's words. Next time, I'd be more careful.

Walt arrived at eight. "I heard the news. Thank goodness Danny found the mayor's killer."

I nodded and then stood. "We've got a festival to celebrate." I traipsed to the field with my camera, fed the animals, and helped set up the petting zoo. My beauties nuzzled me, and I petted them. They'd kept me calm and helped me think. I never dreamed I'd rely on sheep for comfort as much as I relied on my Shepherd for peace.

Once we set up the creatures to entertain the children, I carried my camera to the center of the festival. I snapped photos of the vendors setting up so Laurel could post them and spread the word of the last day.

I approached Marcy Fox as she hung bedazzled t-shirts in her booth. She spun around at the sound of my footsteps. "Lyndie." Before I reached her table, she vaulted toward me and hugged me around the neck. “You saved me.” Word traveled fast in small towns. “I had no idea Johnson, or whoever he pretended to be, killed the mayor.”

“I understand you didn’t, but tell me one thing. How were you connected with the mayor when he lived in Charleston, and why didn’t you leverage him for the business expansion you wanted?” I crossed my arms.

She grasped her hands in front of her and focused on a patch of grass beside her foot, then lifted her chin and scanned my face. “I attended a ball in the city and met him there. We had a photo taken together, and it got published. I didn’t run into him again until he moved here. After the ball, I confided in him about something I wasn’t proud of in my business dealings. I thought I’d never see him again. He held on to the information and held it over my head. Thing is, I’d confessed to the people I’d hurt and made amends, but I didn’t want it brought up again. I’m sorry I didn’t tell you the truth, especially after you rescued me when I got hit on the head.”

“It’s all right. I understand.”

“By the way, Danny told me Johnson is the one who knocked me out. He had planned to steal money, but when you came in, he ran out the back door.”

“I’m glad I came when I did, and I’m happy you’re doing well. Let me take a photo of you and your booth.” She posed for me. “Thanks.” I waved my fingers. “I’m going to check on my aunt.”

At Aunt Cordy's booth, Walt lifted a box of apple butter to the table, and my aunt created a display of the fruit-filled jars. Danny had told her he'd return her apple butter paddle after Mr. Winter's trial. My heart overflowed. Justice prevailed, and my people gathered together to celebrate.

Someone bumped into me from the side. "Hey, Lyndie."

"Zach. Hi. Thanks for all you've done." I side-hugged him.

He hugged me back. "You're welcome."

We stepped apart. "Want to help me deliver bees tonight?"

"Sure."

His eyes searched my face.

"Is there something you want to say?"

He shoved his hair away from his face. "Yeah. I'm thankful Winters didn't hurt you, and I'm glad our sleuthing days are over."

"Yep. Until next time." His forehead wrinkled, and his mouth fell open. Then I winked and grinned.

THE END

Enjoy These Apple Recipes

Cooked Apples

5 medium apples (peeled and diced)

¼ cup of water

Cook down the apples with the water on medium heat until apples are soft, and stir to keep from sticking

Add ¼ cup of dark brown sugar (light brown is good too, but the dark brown gives a rich flavor)

1/8 teaspoon of nutmeg

1/8 teaspoon of cinnamon

A splash of vanilla

Stir

I serve them over hot buttered biscuits.

I used Pink Lady and Honey Crisp Apples.

Crockpot Apple Butter ***contributed by Cathy Griffith***

Yield: 4 cups

This recipe will fill:

· 2 pint jars (16 oz.)

· 4 half pint jars (8 oz.)

· 8 quarter pint jars (4 oz.)

Ingredients:

1 dozen apples, peeled, cored, cubed

½ c water

¼ c brown sugar

½ teaspoon cinnamon

½ tsp all spice.

Directions

1. Put the apples, sugar and spices in a crock pot (4 quarts or larger), cover and cook on high for one hour.

2. Cook on high until the apples are tender and can be easily mashed with a fork, between 4 to 6 hours.

3. Use an immersion blender and puree the apples until they are smooth.

4. Sterilize jars and lids in boiling water for 5 minutes.

5. Fill the jars to within 1/4 inch to the top. Run a knife around the insides of the jars to remove air bubbles.

6. Moisten a paper towel and wipe the rims of each jar.

7. Add the lids and rings to the jars.

8. Place the jars of apple butter in the freezer.

Apple Butter Snack Cake ***contributed by Cathy Griffith***

Ingredients

1 cup all-purpose flour

3/4 cup brown sugar

1 teaspoon baking soda

1/2 teaspoon salt

1/4 teaspoon nutmeg

4 tablespoons butter melted

1 cup apple butter

1 teaspoon vanilla extract

1 egg

1 cup raisins

1/2 to 1 cup walnuts could use pecans

Instructions

In a large bowl whisk together the flour, brown sugar, baking soda, salt and nutmeg.

Stir in the melted butter with a spoon, then add apple butter, vanilla extract, egg, raisins and nuts to batter.

Spray an 8 x 8 baking dish with cooking spray and spread the batter in baking dish.

Bake in preheated 350 degree oven for 35 to 40 minutes or until the center tests done.

Thank you Cathy for the delicious recipes

Apple Bread

Ingredients

2 large eggs

½ cup brown sugar

¾ cup granulated sugar

½ cup vegetable oil

4 teaspoons vanilla extract

2 cups apples, peeled and diced

2 cups all-purpose flour

1 ½ teaspoons salt

1 teaspoon baking powder

1 teaspoon ground cinnamon

Instructions

Preheat the oven to 350°F.

Spray a 9X5 inch loaf pan with cooking spray.

Beat eggs, brown sugar, granulated sugar, vegetable oil, and vanilla extract in a mixing bowl.

Add apples and mix.

Mix flour, salt, baking powder, and cinnamon in a separate bowl.

Add to the apple mixture and stir—just until evenly combined into a thick batter. Pour batter into the prepared loaf pan.

Bake in the preheated oven for 45 minutes.

Then cover loaf pan with aluminum foil; continue baking until a toothpick inserted into the center comes out clean, about 15 minutes more.

Cool in the pan for 10 minutes before removing then cool completely on a wire rack.

Acknowledgements

Writing a book and getting it published takes a boatload of people. Although I write the words, I need everyone who climbs aboard on the writing journey.

I always want to thank God first for his mercy and grace and the amazing gift of writing. Through much prayer and preparation, God has grown me as an author and a person.

What more could I ask of my husband than to support my dreams? That's exactly what he does in every way. Thank you, Tim.

My children, their spouses, and my grandchildren inspire me and encircle me with love and support. I am so blessed to have a supportive family and friends.

A huge thank you goes to my daughter, Maggie, who painted the lovely watercolor cover of this book and designed it. I'm so thankful God has blessed me with talented children who use their gifts for Him.

I'm so grateful to Bev Cinnamon and Jackie Layton for reading the manuscript and giving me input as beta readers, and to Kathleen Friesen for her insightful critiques. I value your wisdom and encouragement, but most of all your friendship.

Kim Garee—my critique partner, editor, and friend. I can't say enough about your hand in helping to shape my drafts into a story. Your patience and knowledge of the written word made this book so much better. Thank you for sticking with me.

A huge thanks to my readers. Without you, I wouldn't keep writing. I've met some wonderful folks along the way and so appreciate your encouragement and support. I hope I continue to write stories you want to read.

I believe God places people in my path to encourage and push me forward. I appreciate each and every one.

About the Author

Penny Frost McGinnis has loved books for as long as she can remember, from sharing a childhood library with her cousins to working in libraries until retirement. An avid reader and lifelong learner, she lives in southwest Ohio with her husband and their golden retriever, Rosie May. Penny embraces her faith, family, and enjoys fiber arts, and baseball. She writes with the goal of encouraging and uplifting her readers.

Find Penny online:

https://www.pennyfrostmcginnis.com/
https://www.facebook.com/PennyFrostMcGinnisAuthor
https://www.instagram.com/pennyfrostmcginnisauthor/

Sign up for Penny's newsletter, to stay in touch and get a free short story on the website https://www.pennyfrostmcginnis.com/

… and to make it your ambition to lead a quiet life: You should mind your own business and work with your hands, just as we told you, so that your daily life may win the respect of outsiders and so that you will not be dependent on anybody.

-1 Thessalonians 4:11-12

Thank you!

If you enjoyed One Rotten Apple, I'd love for you to leave a review on Amazon, Bookbub, or Goodreads. That's the best compliment you can give an author.

You might also enjoy books by:

Kim Garee: https://kimgaree.com/ *romance*

Jackie Layton: https://jackielaytoncozyauthor.com/ *cozy mystery*

Kathleen Friesen: https://kathleenfriesen.weebly.com/ *inspirational fiction*

Books by Penny Frost McGinnis

Abbott Island Series:

#1 Home Where She Belongs

#2 Home Away from Home

#3 Home at Last

Home for Christmas (novella, between 2 & 3)

Picture Books:

Betsy and Bailey: No One Will Be Just Like You

Otto and Ollie: Play Together Everyday

Devotional:

Hope for Today's Heart: Reflections on God's Creation

www.ingramcontent.com/pod-product-compliance
Lightning Source LLC
LaVergne TN
LVHW010643110826
845149LV00014B/2940

* 9 7 9 8 9 9 4 4 7 2 0 1 9 *